P9-APJ-243

LOVING ME THROUGH THE RAIN 3

A Novel By
A'ZAYLER

© 2016

Published by Leo Sullivan Presents
www.leolsullivan.com

All rights reserved.
This is a work of fiction. Names, characters, businesses, places, events and incidents are either the products of the author's imagination or used in a fictitious manner. Any resemblance to actual persons, living or dead, or actual events is purely coincidental. Unauthorized reproduction, in any manner, is prohibited.

A'ZAYLER

Chapter 1: The End or the Beginning?

Rain squinted hard as she tried to look avoid Love's eyes. He was standing at the door of her hospital room staring at her, Summer, and Alex. The three of them had been talking about his sister, Fallon, when he walked in and heard them. Though he'd asked her two times already who she was talking about, she remained still, not saying anything because she wasn't sure what to say.

It wasn't her business to tell. Hell, it really wasn't even her business to know. Fallon hadn't told her, so she was certain she wouldn't want her telling Dakota either. She could slap Summer for being so nosey and telling them what she'd read on Fallon's chart. Rain fidgeted with the covers on her bed but didn't break eye contact.

"Rain, I know you hear me talking to you." Love's voice sounded through the semi-empty hospital room.

"We'll leave y'all alone. Just call me later, boo." Summer stood from the bed and grabbed her purse.

"Why we got to leave?" Alex stayed seated.

Summer pointed her finger at him. "Bitch, get your ass up and come on. Nosey behind."

Alex sucked his teeth and stood from the bed. He stormed over to the chair and grabbed his purse. When he turned around, all three of them were looking at him. Summer and Rain with looks of amusement, Love's face was unreadable, but he probably didn't find Alex the least bit entertaining.

Summer looped her arm through his and shook her head. "You make me so damn sick sometimes."

"Whatever. You wanted to leave. Not me... bye, Rain." Alex waved over his shoulder.

Love stepped to the side so that they could pass him before closing the door and walking over to Rain's bed. Rain's heart was beating a mile a minute as she tried to think of what to do next. Was she supposed to tell him? Was she not supposed to tell him? Should she make up some type of lie to fill in for their outburst? Summer and Alex had just left her; hadn't thought twice about helping her get out of the mess they'd help her make.

Love's locs were in a loose ponytail at the back of his neck. Some of the burgundy ends were hanging over his shoulder and around the top of his arm. He was so handsome with the light scowl on his face. He was seated with his legs stretched out in front of him with one of his hands in his lap and the other resting on her thigh.

"Tell me what's good, Rain. I know it's something you're trying to hard not to tell me."

Rain was thrown off by his tone for a moment because she'd thought he was angry, but it didn't sound like he was. He rubbed her thigh softly, as he looked up at her face. As bad as Rain wanted to look away, she couldn't because he was so beautiful and all hers. The dark chocolate skin and beautiful light brown irises were so magnetic. She couldn't help but stare. He turned his head slightly to the side and softened the look on his face.

Rain could feel herself getting hotter and she hated it. Now was not the time for sex, but he was making it so hard. Being his beautifully handsome self, not doing anything, in particular, just watching her like only he could. Making her forget any and everything around and wanting to just jump into his lap and ride him into the sunset.

"Baby Doll. You okay?"

Rain nodded.

"I heard you say someone had AIDS. Who were you talking about?"

Dang!

Rain held her head down and pushed the hair that had just fallen over her eyes, behind her ear. She took a deep breath and tried to calm her breathing. Love could obviously tell something was wrong with her because he grabbed the bottom of her chin and held her head up. Rain's eyes darted away from his momentarily, but it didn't last as long as she would have liked.

"Look at me."

Rain's eyes landed on his and stayed, her dark ones to his light ones. "Summer."

Love's whole body tensed up. "What?"

Rain palmed her face and bit the inside of her cheek. Why in the hell did she just lie like that?

Love stood up from the bed. "When she found that shit out?"

"Yesterday." *And the lie continued.*

"Damn, that's fucked up. I need to tell my nigga. They been fucking and shit." Love sounded disgusted.

Rain sat back on her bed and tried her hardest not to laugh. Summer was going to kill her. Whenever Love did tell Jacorey, that was going to be some funny shit. Rain giggled quietly because she could imagine how Summer and Jacorey were going to act when it came up. Both of them could be so dramatic at times.

"How in the fuck she missed that shit?" Love turned around and leaned against the windowsill.

Rain shrugged.

"Ain't no way she could have missed no shit like that. That girl is healthy as fuck. Why you playing with me, Rain?" Love's entire demeanor changed.

Rain sighed because she thought that maybe she'd bought herself some time, but clearly that wasn't happening. Love crossed his arms over his chest and looked at her. He didn't smile, nor did he frown. A straight face with not one ounce of emotion was displayed. Time was up. Her game was over.

"Fallon." Her name was a whisper on Rain's lips.

Rain watched him fall apart in front of her. She jumped out of her bed the moment she saw his chest sink in. His arms uncrossed and he grabbed his head with his hands. He sighed heavily before releasing something that sounded like more of a growl than anything. His shoulders rose and fell as he took deep breaths and released tears at the same time.

Rain was about to wrap her arms around his waist, but she was unable to. He had leaned over and had his hands resting on his kneecaps. His ponytail fell to one side of his neck, as he tried to catch his breath. Rain rubbed her hand up and down his back, allowing him time to gather himself. When he began dry heaving, Rain ran to the small wooden stand next to her bed.

She opened one of the drawers and grabbed the plastic pink tub and ran to him. With impeccable timing, Love began to vomit the moment she placed the bucket in front of his face. She held the bucket with one hand and moved his hair out of the way with the other.

"It's okay, baby." Rain tried her best to soothe him.

"Urrgggh," came from his mouth, as he continued to throw up the remnants of his stomach.

When he fell down to his hands and knees, Rain nearly spilled the bucket of vomit. She was trying her best to keep it near his mouth so he wouldn't make a mess, but he was making it hard. On all fours, Love threw up until he had nothing left. Once he finally finished, he sat back on the floor and leaned against the wall. He lay his head back and closed his eyes while Rain stood to empty the bucket.

Once she was finished, she washed her hands and wet a few paper towels to wipe his mouth. She kneeled next to him and cleaned his mouth. He was probably as weak as he felt because he hadn't moved, nor had he tried to offer her any help. His eyes remained closed with his arms down by his side. If she didn't know any better, she would have thought he had fallen asleep.

Rain made sure he was cleaned up before she threw the paper towels away and returned to the floor next to him.

"Get a pillow to sit on," he told her.

Rain smiled and stood to get a pillow. He wasn't too out of it; he remembered to tell her not to sit on the hard floor. The nurse had come in the day before and explained different things, and hemorrhoids were one. She explained to Rain that she should try her best not to sit on anything too hard. Clearly, Love had been listening, too.

She returned with one of the pillows from her bed and sat next to him. Once she was comfortable, she leaned her head over and laid it on his shoulder. She laced her fingers with his and held their hands in her lap.

"I'm sorry, baby."

"How did you know?"

Rain debated lying again but figured she might as well get it all out in the open at one time.

"I went to talk to her."

Love's eyes opened and he turned to look at her. "You did what?"

"I went to her room and talked to her. She's really nice, and the two of you look so much alike."

"Why would you do that, Rain? I didn't tell you to do that."

"Okay, first of all, I didn't need your permission. You're not my daddy. Second of all, because somebody needed to do something. You and her both are walking around in this world like y'all have nobody when you could have each other. I don't understand it. That's crazy as hell."

Love's breathing began to pick up as he listened to her speak about him and his sister's relationship.

"That still doesn't give you the right to go behind my back and talk to her."

Rain leaned forward so that he could see her face. "You must didn't hear me when I just said that you weren't my daddy?"

Love sucked his teeth and looked away from her.

"Now I know you may not want to hear what I have to say because you're all in your feelings right now, but aren't you the same one that was just sitting here vomiting because you found out she's sick? Clearly, there's some love and issues there that need to be addressed." Rain stood up from the floor. "If neither of you are mature enough to handle it then I'll do it for you. I have not one problem doing so."

Rain sat on the edge of her bed and looked at Love. She could understand where he was coming from, but that didn't mean she was going to allow him to throw any unnecessary tantrums. That was his sister and they needed to act as such. Whatever little problems they'd had in the past, it was time for them to let them go.

They were grown, and may not have a lot of time left to spend together, so they needed to spend it wisely. She sat in the same spot looking at him for another few minutes until he began to stand from the floor. When he was at his full height, he stretched his limbs before yawning. After he'd gotten himself together, he walked to the chair he had been sleeping in and took a seat.

Without saying anything to her, he pulled his phone out and began scrolling. Rain thought about saying something to him, but she didn't have the time, nor the patience, so she didn't even bother. If he wanted to act like a butthole because he didn't want her help, then so be it. She would leave him right to it.

She got up from her bed and fumbled around in her purse for her cell phone before sitting back and making herself comfortable again. If he wanted to act like a fool, then she could too. They sat in her room for nearly a whole hour straight without saying anything to one another. The only reason they ended up having to say something was because the nurse came in with her discharge papers.

Rain was over the moon happy. She had been waiting on that since the day she'd gotten there. She was so ready to go, it only took her twenty minutes to get dressed.

"You ready?" Love grabbed the small purple bag with all of her things in it.

"No. I need to stop by your sister's room first." Rain knew that was a low blow, but she didn't care. She liked Fallon and was going to pursue a relationship with her.

If she and Love chose not to have common sense and do the same, then that was their business. Her parents hadn't raised her like that. There was no way in the world she would have a sibling in the same town as her and not talk to them. That was just stupid.

"No, the hell you don't."

"Oh, yes I do, and I will. If you don't want to join me, then please take your butt to the car and I'll be down when I finish."

"Rain, I'm not playing around. You're not going. Let's go."

"Yes, I am."

Love released a frustrated breath and looked toward the door. He took another few deep breaths before grabbing all of her things and storming out of her room. She felt a little dejected because she'd assumed he would have been a little easier to win over. She'd thought a little convincing and sweet talk would have changed his mind. Clearly, that hadn't worked.

For a minute, she almost thought about changing her mind and just going home without seeing Fallon again, but she decided against it. It would only take her a minute to exchange numbers with her. There was no telling when they would run into each other again, so she might as well take advantage of the current opportunity.

Rain checked her face in the mirror, making sure she still looked decent, before sliding her feet into her slippers and looking around her room. She wanted to be sure that she hadn't left anything before exiting. When she was sure she had everything, she left the room and headed back around to Fallon's room.

The door was closed, with the same warning sign on the door. Being that she now knew what was wrong with her, she didn't feel as nervous about going in. Of course, she knocked first, but as soon as she heard Fallon yell for her to come in, she pushed the door open. The same man from earlier was still there, and he was sitting in the chair at the bottom of Fallon's bed.

Rain smiled at him politely before rounding the corner for Fallon to see that it was her. As soon as she saw Rain, she smiled.

"I swear you look just like Dakota. This is crazy." Rain shook her head.

Everything about her face resembled Dakota's. It was so weird looking at his face on a girl. He was so sexy to Rain, but there was nothing sexy about Fallon. Not in Rain's opinion. She was a very beautiful girl, but it was still weird. Or maybe Rain was the weird one.

"He's not with you, is he?" Fallon's eyes got wide.

Rain shook her head. "No. It's just me."

"Good. What made you come back so fast? You missed me already?" Fallon smiled, and the hazel eyes that matched Dakota's twinkled.

Rain shared in her giggling. "Of course, I missed you, but that's not why I came back. They finally discharged me so I wanted to come by and maybe exchange numbers or something before I go home. Maybe we could have lunch or something one day."

Fallon's smile dropped a little, but she nodded her head. "I don't normally get out of the house much, but sure. We can talk on the phone."

Rain noticed the way she looked over at her man before agreeing to exchange numbers. Though she wasn't a big fan of that, it wasn't her business, so she just pulled her phone out and waited for Fallon to call her number out to her. After she had it entered in her phone, she called the number and heard a phone ringing.

Fallon looked over at her phone on the table next to her bed and picked it up. "I'll save it. It was so nice to meet you, Rain. You seem so sweet. I'm glad my brother has you."

Rain touched her chest where her heart was. "I wish he had you, too."

Fallon nodded before looking away. Rain took that as a sign to leave well enough alone. "Well, I'll be hitting you up soon, sis."

Rain stuck her phone back in her pocket and let herself out of the room. She wanted to hug her or something, but she wasn't wearing any of the protective gear that was recommended, so she didn't bother. She walked back around the corner where her room was so that she could head to the elevators. When she rounded the corner, Love was leaning against the wall with his hands in his pockets.

He saw her and stood straight up on his feet. Rain was caught off guard momentarily by his outstretched hand. Versus continuing on with her attitude, she decided to take his truce and move on. She locked her hands with his and walked down the hallway. They didn't say anything to one another, just proceeded to the exit in silence.

His truck was pulled to the front near the door when they got outside. He helped her inside before rounding the truck and getting in himself. He drove out of the parking lot and in the direction of his home before saying anything.

"You're going to need some clothes," he whispered.

It was like everything that she had been trying not to think about came back in that moment. She hadn't thought about her home being burned down in a few days because it was too painful. That one statement had resurfaced every piece of pain that she had been feeling. It was going to take too much for her to start over, but from the looks of things, she had no other choice. Rain sniffed hard enough to stop any tears from falling.

She cleared her tightening throat as well. "Can we go by there, please?"

Love looked at her and shook his head. "I don't think that's a good idea right now. You just got out of the hospital."

"Please. I want to see it."

She was certain it was against his better judgment, but Love made a U-turn in the middle of the street and drove toward her house. The soft sounds of Jeremih sounded throughout the truck as he drove. Rain looked out of the window, taking in the scenery. It felt so good to be out of the hospital. The various houses and restaurants had her so caught up that she didn't even notice they were in her neighborhood until she saw the blackened building that was once her home.

Tears rose as Love pulled his truck to a stop. Rain unbuckled her seatbelt and opened the door. She was out of the car and headed up her small sidewalk before Love caught up with her. The door was burned to ashes, so she was able to walk right in. With Love's assistance, she moved through the living room. Her furniture was still recognizable, as well as some of her pictures.

She held her stomach when she noticed the picture of her, Alex, and Summer at the hair show, along with the one of just her and Summer on the beach. The corners were slightly burned, but they were still in pretty good shape.

"Can we get all of my stuff that's not burned up?"

Love nodded his head.

"When?"

"Now. Please."

"We can try to get whatever we can, but we're going to need something to put it in."

Rain looked around and walked toward the stairs. She wanted to walk up them, but some of the stairs were missing.

Love ran up behind her and grabbed her wrist. "Let me help you before you fall."

He bent down so she could climb on his back. She was a little slow to get on, but once she was on him and comfortable, he took the stairs, skipping a few, and barely stepping on others until he was at the top. Instead of putting her down, he continued to her room, stepping over burned debris and broken decorations.

Love could feel Rain's tears on his neck and hear her sniffles in his ear, but he knew this would come. It had been the same way with him when he'd first come back to check everything out the day after the fire. The place he'd claimed as his second home for months now, was gone. As if that hadn't made him emotional enough, thinking about her not having made it out was even worse.

It was like a nightmare that he'd woken up from. He squeezed his arms a little tighter around her thighs, just happy that she was still there with him. Once in her bedroom where the fire had started, Rain really broke down. There was absolutely nothing left. Everything that could have possibly been salvaged was gone. It was black, and still a tad bit smoked out.

Due to the fact that her roof had burned down, fresh air had time to circulate throughout the room.

"Let's just go."

That was all Love needed to hear because he hadn't wanted to come in the first place. He turned back around and followed the path they'd used to come in, to go back out. When they were finally back outside, he walked her to the side of his truck before putting her back on her feet. She stood on the side of the truck in her pajamas, waiting for him to unlock the doors.

Love could see that she was on the verge of losing it, so he did the best he could to reassure her. He leaned on his truck with both of his hands on either side of her body. She stood in front of him with her arms crossed over her chest. Her eyes were wet and her face a little red from crying. Love leaned down some so that they were face to face.

"It's going to be okay. You know that, right?"

Rain shook her head.

"Yes, it is. I got you, baby. No matter what."

"What about when we break up?" She sniffed.

"What about when we break up? Fuck all that, we ain't breaking up. We gon always be together."

Rain smiled. "That's what your mouth says."

"Hell, that's what my dick says too." He laughed when she punched him in the chest. "But for real, I'm here for you. I ain't going nowhere. We'll be fine. When you get mad at me, just go to your sister's house for an hour or so and come back home."

Rain really laughed at that. She could tell he was doing all that he could to make her feel better, and it was actually helping. Her eyes wandered over his shoulder again and observed the damage to her house, before looking back at his face.

"What about the person who did this?"

"Don't worry about that. I'll take care of that too."

Rain had no idea how he planned to do that, but she was exhausted and ready to go so she just nodded her head and stepped to the side so that he could open the door for her. When she turned around, he kissed the exposed part of her shoulder and pulled her backward into him. His large hand slid across her abdomen and rested there.

"Y'all gon be straight. Aight?"

"Aight."

Love kissed the side of her face before opening the door and helping her in. She situated herself comfortably and stared at the pile of ashes and burned materials until they pulled away. As frustrating as it was to have no place to call home anymore, it was even more frustrating to not know the reason why. She had no idea who the woman was or why she would do something like that. That fact alone had shattered her peace of mind. Hopefully living with Love wouldn't be too bad.

After leaving her house, Love drove her to Kmart to get some clothes and then to the park down the street from his job. They were having another community service function for the children of the community. There were two fire trucks, a few police, and a couple of ambulances parked on the grass in the center of the park. Love had already told her about it and figured it would be a good outing to take her mind off of things.

Initially, Rain hadn't wanted to go, but being that she was fresh out of the hospital, she could use the fresh air. The purple racerback dress and sandals she wore was the perfect outfit. It was cute and casual, without doing too much. Love had done a good job picking it out. She was a tad hesitant when he'd first volunteered to go in the store and get her something to put on. Now she was actually impressed.

Her hair was in a long air-dried ponytail, and she wore a pair of gold hoop earrings that he'd brought out of the store as well. Rain held his hand as they walked deeper onto the grass. He looked around, making sure to help her as they stepped over the rocks. She didn't need anything else going wrong, including a minor slip up at the park.

There were plenty of people already surrounding the area with the kids as they approached. The closer they got, the more nervous she became, for some reason. She wasn't sure if it was just her or not, but it felt like everyone was looking at her. She tried to ignore it, but she couldn't.

"Why is everybody staring at us?"

"They're not, Rain. Relax, baby."

She nodded, and he squeezed her hand a little tighter for reassurance. "Even if they are staring, which they're not, they have every reason to." He kissed the side of her head. "You're the prettiest thing out here."

Rain smiled like a giddy schoolgirl at his compliment. "Thank you."

"No thanks needed. Just try to enjoy yourself today." Love pulled her behind him as he finally got to his truck and team.

They all greeted her warmly, some even stopping to give her a hug and express their thoughts and kind words. The whole thing was nice, and she definitely appreciated it. After she walked around the entire group, still holding Love's hand, he escorted her to a cement picnic table.

"Sit here and relax. I have to go help the children on the truck and stuff... You okay?"

"I'll be fine. You go ahead."

He kissed her lips and walked away. Rain sat back and watched all of the people coming and going as the hours passed. Love was so gentle and loving with the kids. It made her smile just thinking about how he was going to be with their little one. She was busy basking in the joyous thoughts of her life further down the road when a group of people caught her eye. Well, a few of the faces in particular.

Stacey, Damien, and two other men she'd seen around Love before. They were coming down the hill with their children and two women. One of the women was Unique. Rain was about to wonder what she was doing there until she saw the little girl walking beside her. Apparently, they'd been invited to the family day out as well.

Well, most of them probably had been. She was almost positive Stacey had invited himself. Rain watched them until they got closer to her, then she turned away. Not only was she in no mood to speak, but her body was in no condition to fight. From the type of person Unique was, she could already tell that if she walked over there, it was going to be some shit.

Rain looked down at her phone and went to her Snapchat. Maybe that would entertain her long enough for her not to have to speak. When she felt a hand on the back of her elbow, she knew she'd have no such luck. Rain looked up and Stacey was standing there. Out of all the people that could have bothered her, it had to be him.

She was actually starting to think that she would have much rather it be Unique's sneaky ass. She frowned as she looked up at him.

"What?"

"Damn, it's like that?"

"What do you want, Stacey?" Rain observed the black eye and long bruise on the side of his face. Apparently somebody had gotten to him before she could. *Good for his ass.*

"I didn't come over here to disturb your day or anything like that, I just wanted to tell you that I apologize for any confusion that I may have caused. It wasn't my intention to stir up any bullshit."

"I can't tell. You sure didn't try to fix it once you noticed it was getting out of hand."

Stacey shrugged his shoulders. "My fault, Rain. I was really feeling you, and I let that shit go to my head."

"You did, but it's cool."

"So you really feeling Love like that?"

Rain frowned. "Stacey, you said you was sorry or whatever, now go 'head on now before you start some more shit."

"Boy, what the fuck you doing over here?" Love's voice made them both jump.

Stacey held his hands up in surrender. "Just apologizing, my nigga. Nothing more."

Love looked at Rain. "That's what it is?"

Rain nodded her head.

"Cool." Love dapped Stacey up before watching him walk away.

Once he was gone, Love turned back around and placed his hands on both sides of Rain. He was so close to her face that their noses were nearly touching.

"What that nigga say?"

"What happened to his face?" Rain challenged.

Love looked away. "I don't know. I guess somebody caught his ass."

"Um huh."

"For real." Love fixed the fly away hair from her ponytail.

"I wonder was that a certain somebody I know." Rain pushed further.

"Hell, you should have told me it was a woman sooner." Love kissed her again before winking and walking away.

Rain shook her head and followed him with her eyes as he got back to his truck. Her line of vision fell directly upon Unique. They stared at one another as everything went on around them. Initially, Rain was unsure if Unique knew who she was, but judging by the way she was looking at her, it was clear that she did.

She didn't look angry or annoyed, or anything like that, just curious. The way her eyes wandered over Rain, she appeared to be trying to look through her. Maybe she wanted to see what it was about Rain that Dakota loved so much. That conclusion was obvious because had it been Rain in Unique's position, that's what she would have been doing.

"What you doing sitting over here by yourself?" a male voice made her turn her head from Unique.

Damien? Rain was a bit surprised that he was talking to her because for as long as she'd known him to be dealing with Alex, he hadn't said more than two words to her. Unlike the first night she met him, when she and Summer had accompanied Alex to his friend Connie's house. He was all smiles that night.

That was before Rain became privy to his secret. It had been unspoken since then that they weren't friends.

"I'm just chilling. Waiting on Dakota to finish."

Damien looked a little bit fidgety as he took the seat next to her on the table. He looked around them, checking behind them and both sides, before leaning his head closer to hers.

"I know what you might think of me, but that ain't me, shawty. I fuck with your friend and everything, but it ain't on no gay shit. I just like him or whatever."

"I honestly don't think nothing of you. You like what you like. That ain't got nothing to do with me."

"Nah, nah, nah. I know how y'all girls are and shit."

Rain was a little lost on what his whole plan was for coming to talk to her, so she tried to figure it out. "Okay, Damien, what's going on? Why are you over here talking to me about something you clearly aren't comfortable talking about?"

He sighed and looked around again. Rain didn't understand him. If something made you that uncomfortable, you had no business trying to discuss it in a park full of people.

"I just want you to holla at your friend for me. He on some ole bitch shit right now. Wanting me to leave my girl and shit, and I can't do that."

Damien rubbed his hand over his face, and for the first time since Alex had been dealing with him, Rain could see why. His posture, his attitude, his movements, everything about him at that moment, screamed he was in love. He looked nervous or worried about him and Alex's relationship, or whatever they called it.

"What you want me to do?"

"Just tell him to give me some time. This shit ain't easy for me. I ain't gay, I just like fucking him."

Rain sucked her teeth. "Nigga, my friend deserves more than somebody that just likes to fuck. You think he ain't got other niggas for shit like that? Furthermore, he has people that genuinely want to be with him. You seriously think I'm going to tell him to sit around and wait on you to give him sloppy seconds?" Rain sucked her teeth and looked away.

Damien blew out a frustrated breath. "I see why y'all friends. You're just as much drama as his ass."

Rain smiled and shrugged. "I love him."

Damien looked her in her eyes. "I do, too."

Rain's heart just melted at that moment. She'd been the main one encouraging Alex to leave him alone, but now she saw why he couldn't. They had a real deal thing going on, with love actually being a big part of it.

"Awwww," Rain wrapped her arm around Damien's neck and pulled him playfully into a hug. "That's so sweet."

Damien laughed and pulled away. "Just tell him for me. He won't answer my calls."

Rain picked her phone up from beside her and scrolled through it before calling Alex on FaceTime. "Hold on, I'm about to call him. You don't have to say anything if you don't want to. I'll just let you see him." She then pulled her headphones out and handed him one while she kept the other. "No one can hear us. If someone comes, I'll just hang up on him... cool?"

Damien looked around again before nodding his head. A few seconds later, Alex's face popped up on the screen. He had big curls in his weave and his face was beat to death with his makeup. As always, he looked fabulous and better than most women. From his surroundings and how made up he was, it was clear that he was at work. It looked like his phone was propped up on something because he wasn't holding it, but she could still see him head on.

"Hey, babyyy." He looked into the phone. "You okay?"

"Yeah, I'm good. I have a surprise for you real quick."

Alex looked from the person's hair he was doing and picked his phone up. "Oooh what bitch? You know I love surprises."

Rain smiled before turning her camera so that Damien's face was now in the screen. Alex turned his nose up and rolled his eyes.

"I should hang up on your skinny ass."

"Why you being mean? He just wanted to see you."

"If he wants to do that then he needs to leave that secret baby mama of his and come where I'm at."

"You busy today?" Damien asked.

"Yep."

"Alex," Rain pleaded.

Alex sighed before shaking his head. "I take lunch in an hour."

"Meet me somewhere."

"Whatttt? You want to be in public with me?"

"I love you."

Rain melted again, and from the looks of things, so did Alex. He fought the smile tugging at his lips. "I love you, too. I'm going home for lunch."

"Bet." Damien winked and Rain turned the phone back on her.

"I'mma kill your punk ass."

"Shut up, bitch, you love me." Rain smiled at him just as a little boy ran up to them and grabbed Damien's leg.

"Come on, Daddy, it's our turn."

Rain's eyes got wide then she looked at Damien, who shrugged and got up from the bench. He grabbed the little boy's hand and looked over his shoulder at Rain once more, before walking away to the group he'd come with. The other girl who had been with Unique was now looking at her, but for some reason, Rain didn't think that was Damien's baby mama.

Aside from the girl hanging on one of the other men all day, she was almost positive that Damien wouldn't have come over there to her if his baby mama were there. Not in the mood to deal with any females or their uncalled for drama, Rain turned away from the girl and focused her attention back on Love and the children he was with.

Sitting back watching Damien interact with his son was so weird to her. It was like he was living a double life or something. On one hand, he was every female's dream, then on the other, he was a nigga on the down low. A small shiver ran through Rain's body as she entertained the thought. It was wrong on so many different levels.

No woman in her right mind would assume, let alone believe that Damien had just been professing his love for another man. How easy was it to be fooled? Rain shook her head at the thought. There were probably so many men like Damien floating around. For a reason she didn't know, her eyes wondered to Love.

Just as quick as she thought about it, she dismissed it. He gave no signs of it, and she would flat out kill him. Simple as that. No ifs, ands, or buts about it. Love would be dead as he had to die if she found out he was on the down low. After thinking about it for another few seconds, she had to laugh at herself.

The day went by rather quickly, a lot quicker than she'd expected, and before she knew it, she was on the way home with Dakota. He was driving with one hand and holding her leg with the other.

"How you feeling, beautiful?"

"Blessed."

Love looked at her and smiled. "Me too."

For the rest of their ride home, Rain thought about how blessed she was to have escaped that house with her life. To make things even better, God had blessed her with a man who would risk his own life for hers. Now that was something she would never get tired of.

Chapter 2: Friends Forever

Love lay awake on the sofa watching Rain sleep. She was snoring lightly, and one of her arms was thrown above her head. She was lying on her side in front of him with her mouth slightly open. They had stopped to pick up some food for dinner before going back to his house. It wasn't long after they'd finished eating that Rain was asleep.

It had been a little over two hours since she'd fallen asleep and he was debating on whether to wake her up or not. He wanted to talk and just enjoy her company, but he also wanted her to get the rest he knew she needed. It was nearing nine o'clock, and she would probably be up half the night, but if that was the case, then he was cool with it.

Love had called Summer earlier when Rain had first fallen asleep so that she could run a quick errand for him before coming over. She, Alex, and Jacorey would all be stopping by in a few seconds to play cards and stuff, so she would get it then. Love knew all of this had to be hard on her, so he was making an effort to do whatever he could to make things easier.

He too was stressed because whatever crazy ass bitch that had done it was still on the loose. He needed to find out whoever it was before they tried to attack her again. Now that she was pregnant with his baby, he wanted to be extra careful with her. Not that he hadn't before, but especially now. He'd tried to think of every woman that he could think of and the only one that kept popping into his head was Unique.

The only thing about that was he didn't think she was crazy enough to do no shit like that, nor did he think she cared enough. He and Unique hadn't had anything going on, so why would she want to harm Rain? Sure she'd made a few jealous remarks about her, but what woman wouldn't? That was common shit that came up between women.

Somebody trying to burn his girl's house down with her in it required some type of serious hatred. Who in their right mind would hate Rain? She was the sweetest female he'd ever encountered. Surely she was this way with everybody. Love looked over at her when he noticed movement from her body. She was squirming and her face was frowning.

Love watched her until she opened her mouth and screamed. He jumped to the sofa she was lying on and shook her lightly. When she didn't wake up, he sat her whole body up and leaned her head against his chest.

"Wake up, baby."

Rain stirred a little before opening her eyes and realizing where she was. Her face frowned momentarily, before relaxing again. She wiped her eyes and looked down at the floor with her hand on her forehead.

"You okay?"

"Yeah, I'm cool."

"What happened?"

"It was a fire again, but this time, I was stuck in the shower instead of under the bed."

Love pushed her hair out of her face and kissed her forehead. "It's all right, boo. I'm here." He stood up and grabbed the empty food containers on his way into the kitchen. "You feel like having some company?"

Rain looked at him with her eyebrows scrunched together. "It depends on who it is?"

"Your sister, that nigga, and Jacorey."

Rain laughed. "Why you always have to exclude Alex like that?"

"Because I just don't understand why he parades around like a lil bitch, instead of a nigga. That shit just doesn't make any sense to me."

"That's just who he is. He's my best friend. He's actually kind of like my other sister, so you really should try to fix your attitude when it comes to him."

"I don't do nothing to him."

"Well, you talk about him bad enough. Stop it. He's nice and he loves me."

Love looked around the living room before going into the kitchen. "Yeah," was all he said.

He loved Rain and could feel where she was coming from, but he still didn't understand that nigga and his preferences. What man in their right mind wouldn't want some pussy? That just didn't make sense to him. But whatever. That was his shit, so he would leave him to it. He didn't have to deal with the nigga like that, so whatever.

He threw their trash away and joined her back in the living room. She was lying back on the sofa watching TV when he sat down.

"So, why is everyone coming over?"

Love shrugged. "Just to give us something to do. I don't want you sitting around looking all sad and shit, so I invited them. Maybe we can play cards or something."

"Aww, well ain't you the sweetest thing?"

"I try to be."

"You are."

Rain leaned her head on his shoulder and he gripped her thigh. Just when he was about to ask her for some kisses, the doorbell rang. He already knew who it was, so he got right up and opened it. Summer and Alex came in with a big purple gift bag and two smaller white bags. He could tell by the white bags that it was the hot wings he'd told them to pick up. The gift bag was the surprise he had for Rain.

"Wake up, bitch, it's the first of the month," Alex sang playfully, as he walked into the kitchen with the bags.

Summer, on the other hand, flopped down on the sofa with the large purple bag in her hand and extended it out to Love.

Love grabbed it from her and held it down by his side. "I almost thought you were going to give it to her."

"I should have, as much trouble as I went through to get it."

"Girl, stop your shit. You ain't have to do nothing but go pick it up. I had already ordered and paid for it."

Summer sucked her teeth. "The hell you say. I had to go to a totally different Wal-Mart because the one you sent it to didn't have it. Now what kind of mess is that?"

Love's face frowned because that really was stupid. "On the website they said they had it."

"Well, that website lied, boo." Summer kicked her shoes off and propped her feet up on the table.

"I just love how y'all sitting here talking about my gift like I'm not sitting here."

Alex walked back into the living room and sat on the other side of them. "How you know it's yours? It could be for his other girlfriend."

"I know right. It could be for the bitch that almost blew your lil skinny ass up."

Everybody in the room looked at Summer. She held her hands up in the air and smiled. "I'm only playing y'all, damn."

Alex burst out laughing. Rain and Love on the other hand didn't find anything funny.

"It's a joke, bitch. Lighten up." Alex tapped Rain's arm, playfully.

"That junk ain't funny. I don't know why y'all think it is."

Summer rolled her eyes and looked at Alex. "She gets on my nerves always being so dramatic. She knows we're just playing with her."

"Ain't it. She makes me sick." Alex chimed in.

"That just ain't shit to play with," Love told them both.

Summer and Alex looked at each other and burst out laughing again. "Man, both of them got a stick up their butt. We might need to leave because clearly they're not in the mood to be playing."

"No we're not either. You and I can laugh. We don't need them." Alex pushed his weave over his shoulder.

Rain rolled her eyes at both of them before reaching for the bag in Love's hand. He smiled at her and pulled it away so that she couldn't reach it.

"Bae, stop playing."

He smiled and handed her the bag. She wasted no time pulling the contents out. Her mouth fell open and she screamed when she saw the picture of the purple touch screen HP computer. She'd been in tears for two days straight, at the hospital, after realizing that hers had been lost in the fire.

"Oh my God!" she yelled, as she clutched the box to her chest. "Kotaaaa," She smiled up at him. "Thank you."

"It's all love, baby doll. You deserve it. Your old one was fucking up anyway."

Rain jumped from the sofa and hugged him as tight as she could with one arm, being that she was still holding onto her computer with the other hand. He grabbed her in both arms and lifted her from the ground.

"Does that mean I get some play tonight? Because your ass been stingy since that damn fire."

Rain giggled into his neck before releasing him. "Yeah, I guess so."

"You guess so? Girl please. You better bust that lil pussy open for that damn boy." Alex had everybody in the room laughing at that comment.

"Listen to your friend, nih. That's all I'm saying." Love was still laughing when he heard the doorbell ring. "Go put you some clothes on."

He nodded his head toward his bedroom and Rain took off for the stairs. When he opened the door, Jacorey walked in with a smaller lavender colored bag. They dapped each other up before Love stepped to the side and allowed him in. He handed him the gift bag on his way inside. He was about to say something to Love, but he changed his mind once he saw Summer.

"Damn, lil sexy ass girl. Why you ain't tell me you was coming through?"

Summer blushed. "I thought Love told you."

"Nah, that nigga ain't tell me nothing. He told me to pick this shit up and bring it here for Rain. He ain't tell me nothing about my best friend being here."

Jacorey walked into Love's living room and took a seat next to Summer. Alex looked over at them and turned his nose up.

"Why y'all ain't tell me this was about to be date night? I would have brought my lil boo."

"It ain't a date night. I just wanted her to chill with her people and have a good time, that's all."

"Um huh. You could have invited one of your homeboys to keep me company."

Love and Jacorey both shot him deadly looks. Jacorey was the only one to speak, though. "Ain't none of our niggas gay, so that shit is dead."

Alex and Summer squealed in humor. "That's a lie."

Jacorey and Love's attention was piqued. Love even walked back into the living room and took a seat on the table. "Man, y'all fucking lying."

"Alex may do a lot of foul shit, but lying on a straight nigga ain't one. If he says your ass is gay, then your ass is fucking gay, my nigga. Ain't no beating around the bush with that." Summer filled them in.

"Why you had to add all that 'he may do a lot of foul shit' mess in? Bitch, don't do me."

Summer and Alex laughed again, totally ignoring the fact that Jacorey and Love were both still waiting for an answer about their friends. It took the two of them a minute to stop playing and laughing, but once they saw the eager looks on the guys faces, they began laughing again.

Jacorey stood up and walked toward the kitchen. "Man, I ain't fucking with y'all."

"You may not be, but one of your homies is," Alex said.

"I don't give a fuck which one of those niggas is fucking you. I just know his ass better not be fuckin' Summer. That's all I know."

Summer waved her hand at him. "Boy, gone in that kitchen."

Jacorey looked her up and down before walking away. "You know what's up."

Just as he left the room, Rain came hopping down the stairs. She was dressed in a pair of yoga pants and a tank top. Her hair was still in her ponytail and her face was bare, minus her glasses. With no hesitation, she walked directly to Love and kissed his lips again before grabbing the new bag from his hand.

As she'd done the last one, she opened it quickly. She pulled out a pack of pens with four new notebooks. One was blue with raindrops on it; the others were metallic red and gold, with the last one having the words *Love Me Through the Rain* airbrushed on it. Her eyes got big as saucers as she stared at the books.

"Dakota Love! Oh my God. I love you." She held the notebooks to her chest before jumping on him again. "You're so amazing, babe."

"You deserve it." He pecked her forehead before walking past and slapping her butt.

"Aight, let's get this show on the road. Who got first?" Summer stood up with the deck of cards in her hand.

"Me and Jacorey." Love followed her to the table.

"Cool. Come on, Alex." She sat down and motioned for Alex to sit across from her.

Cards had never been Rain's thing, so she grabbed all of her new stuff and took a seat on the sofa instead. She pulled the notebook with her and Love's names on the front to the top and opened the pack of pens. He watched her push her glasses on her face before she began writing. He didn't say anything at first, just watched her do her thing.

"What you writing, bae?"

"Another story for you." She smiled up at him. "This notebook will be for us."

Love winked at her before holding his head down. She was the only person in the world who knew how much that meant to him. He'd never told anyone outside of Unique's nosey ass how much he loved reading the stories Rain wrote for him. The only reason she'd gotten that piece of information was because she'd practically taken it. That was a secret between him and Rain, and that's how he planned to keep it.

He was about to blow her a kiss but her head was already down, so he walked to the table and sat down. Alex was already seated across from Summer, with Jacorey sitting across from him. Summer began dealing the cards as soon as he sat down.

"So, which one of my niggas is a sissy, Alex?" Love asked him.

"Wait, let me pour me a shot first. I can't handle this conversation sober." Jacorey stood up from the table and disappeared into the kitchen.

He was holding four shot glasses and a bottle of Cîroc when he returned. He slid each one of them a glass before pouring himself a shot. They passed the bottle around the table until each of their glasses was filled.

"Love, you got a room for me here tonight because I don't drink and drive?" Summer asked, before placing her shot glass to her lips.

"You know it, sis."

"Cool." Summer threw her shot back and poured herself another one.

"Don't get sloppy, bitch, because I ain't told your ass I was staying here tonight." Alex looked at her across the table.

"You can take my car. Jacorey can take me home if you get ready before I do." Summer looked at Jacorey. "Best friend, you got me?"

Jacorey drank his shot. "I got you all right. I got this hard dick for you if you want that."

Summer blushed and picked up her hand of cards. "I'm not about to play with you tonight."

"Y'all don't need to be drinking anyway," Rain yelled from where she was sitting.

"Don't try to spoil our fun because you can't have none." Love looked over his shoulder at her.

Rain smiled. "It's your fault anyway."

"Proud of it." Love told her, as he threw his card down.

For the next few hours, the friends sat around drinking and playing cards. By the time twelve o'clock hit, everybody at the table was drunk and talking junk to one another. Jacorey and Summer being the worse ones. Every other thing that left their mouth was slick. Rain was still writing and had a lot more she could have jotted down had she not heard Alex getting ready to tell all of him and Damien's business.

"I mean, I don't be fucking him. He just does me and I guess he doesn't think that makes him gay."

"If there's any fucking going on between you and another nigga, that's gay. Period. It don't matter who's doing the fucking. The shit is fuckin' gay," Jacorey told Alex.

"That's the same thing I told y'all friend, but he doesn't believe me. Y'all should talk to him and see what the fuck he be thinking about."

"Tell us who he is and we will," Love told him.

"Okay. That's enough. It's time for y'all to stop drinking." Rain walked over to the table and removed the bottle from Alex's hand.

All eyes were on her as she took their drinks from them. Summer was drunk, but she knew what Rain was doing. She smiled at her and winked to express her gratitude. Alex would be thanking her just the same in the morning when he woke up.

"Rain, you are not my mama." Alex pointed at her stomach. "You are that little baby's mama. Not mine. I can drink as much as I want. Ain't that right, Love?"

Just as drunk as Alex was, Love nodded his head.

Rain turned and looked at him. "You need to just go upstairs and lay down. You're ridiculous right now."

"I'll go if you go." He smiled up at her.

"Okay, you go ahead, I'm coming. Let me help them get settled first."

Love pushed himself back from the table and leaned down to Rain. He grabbed her face and kissed her mouth. He kissed her with as much passion as his drunkenness would allow, before stumbling up the stairs to his room. *One down, three more to go.* Rain looked at Alex and figured he should be next. There was no telling what would start coming out of his mouth.

"Come on." She grabbed his hand and pulled him into the living room. "Take your shoes off while I get you some cover."

Rain walked up the stairs and grabbed a sheet, blanket, and pillow from Love's hall closet. When she got back, Alex was sitting on the edge of the sofa with his shoes off. He was looking around the corner at Summer and Jacorey. Summer was seated on his lap kissing him like there was no tomorrow. Rain shook her head and continued to Alex. She would worry about them later.

"Ummm un. Summer has way too much ass to be on his lap like that. Look at it. It's all over his legs. You can't even see his pants no more." Alex snickered. "Look at her, Rain. Her big butt self. That don't make no sense. Ooohhh they nasty, Rain, look. Jacorey has his hands all over her ass. He squeezing it and shit. Oh, they are too much. Get it Summer!" Alex was talking nonstop.

Rain tried to hurry as fast as she could to lay Alex's covers out before Summer and Jacorey forgot that they were in the room. She'd done like Alex had said and looked over her shoulder at them and he wasn't lying. They were damn near having sex already with all the touching and rubbing they were doing on one another.

"You better go give Love some. Don't let that fast bitch be the only one fucking tonight." Alex lay back on the sofa and pulled the covers over him. "Where you taking them to?"

Rain looked at Alex. "Who?"

"Summer and Jacorey."

"The guest room. Why?"

"Because, bitch, I wanted to watch, but my head hurting too bad to be going up those stairs. I'll have to catch them next time."

"Go to sleep, Alex."

"Yes ma'am, Mommy." Alex flipped over on the sofa so that his back was to her and she flipped the lamp off.

Now on to the porn stars in the dining room. Rain stood still, a bit shocked at the way they were carrying on. Summer was now laid back on the table with Jacorey standing between her legs. He was lying on top of her and kissing her neck with her legs wrapped around his waist.

"I don't know where y'all think y'all at, but not up in here." Rain pulled at Summer's legs, making them drop from Jacorey's waist.

He stood up and looked at Rain with a smile. His face was bright, and it was more than clear that he was drunk. He stepped back a few steps before pulling Summer up. She smiled at Rain and hopped down off of the table. When she was on her feet, Jacorey grabbed her hand and pulled her behind him.

"You know where you going, Jacorey?"

"Come on now, Rain. I used to crash here before you did."

"Alright now. Don't y'all be in there being all loud."

Summer held her finger to her lips as she walked up the stairs behind Jacorey. "Shhhh."

"Don't shush me, heffa. Just take your drunk butt up those stairs and go to sleep."

Summer smiled at her sister before turning around and following Jacorey into the second bedroom across from Love's. Rain looked around the room, making sure everything was good, before flipping off the lights and going upstairs. Like she figured he would be, when she when she got into Love's room, he was asleep.

She wasn't really tired because she'd just woken up from a nap, but she got into bed anyway. Her body could still use the rest. The moment she removed her tights and slid beneath the sheets with Love, he rolled over and wrapped his arm around her waist. He pulled her back across the bed until her back was pressed against his chest.

He kissed the back of her neck a few times. "What you want to name the baby?"

"I don't know yet. If it's a boy, we can do a junior if you want."

"Nah, give him his own identity. He might not like this white boy shit anyway."

"I love your name."

"And I love you."

Rain held his hand up and kissed the back of it. "I love you too, Kota."

She closed her eyes and lay still. Before long, she could hear him snoring. She'd thought he might have stayed up at least a little while longer, but she was so wrong. The liquor had him knocked out immediately. His breathing had changed and his grasp on her had loosened some. With a mind full of thoughts, Rain opened her eyes and looked around the dark room.

She wasn't looking at anything in particular; she just couldn't keep her eyes closed. She could hear the faint sounds of Jacorey and Summer's sexual rendezvous, which made her laugh. She couldn't wait to make fun of her when they woke up. Though every one of them were now drunk and asleep, Rain was grateful for her friends and family. They'd cared enough to come over and chill, just to make sure she was feeling all right.

Things like that didn't happen often, so she had to make sure she expressed her thanks when they all woke up. If Love had enough food, she would thank them with breakfast. Rain rolled her eyes at the thought. He probably didn't have anything. Living with him was definitely about to take some getting used to.

Chapter 3: Bad Decisions

"I Want You" by Lloyd blasted through Alex's apartment as he moved around cleaning up. He hadn't been in the mood to do much of anything for the past few days since the fire at Rain's house. Today was the first day he had felt good enough to clean. He had been cleaning since his feet had hit the floor that morning, washing clothes and all.

It had been a little over two hours, and he'd just finished mopping when he heard a knock on the door. He thought about not answering it but went ahead anyway. As soon as his door swung open, Damien walked in and grabbed him. Alex pushed back out of his grasp and closed the door.

"What have I told you about just popping up over here?"

"What have I told you about starting some shit every time I come over here?"

Alex rolled his eyes and went back into the kitchen. He bent over to grab the mop and bucket when Damien stepped up behind him. He made sure to press the hardness in his jeans against Alex's butt.

"You feeling generous?"

"You feeling gay?"

Damien sucked his teeth and cursed. "Why you always on that shit, man? Why can't I ever just come over here and chill with you without all this damn attitude. This is why I won't be with your ass now."

"Nah, nigga, you won't be with me because you can't be with me. It ain't because of my attitude. You love this shit."

Damien stepped to him again and grabbed him. "I damn sure do. Now you fucking or what?"

Alex looked around his living room, trying to think about it. He had promised himself that he would stop accepting anything that Damien chose to hand out, but he always made it so hard. Like that day Rain had called him and they met for lunch. Like always, they laid up until it was time for Damien to dip. Alex had felt neglected that day, just like he did right then. Damien was dressed, fresh haircut and he smelled good. Just the sight of him had Alex ready. That was until it dawned on him that he was extra fresh.

"Hold up. Where you about to go?"

Damien looked down. "It's my baby mama's birthday. We're going to the movies."

"Well, what you doing over here?"

"I wanted to see you." Damien cleared his throat. "I needed to see you."

Stuff like that was what kept Alex holding on. It was like no matter what Damien did, he was always pulling him back with his words.

"She wants me, but I want you." Damien kissed the side of Alex's face. "You can't show me how much you've been missing me before I go?"

"So you want to fuck me before you go with this girl? Why not just fuck her? I'm sure since it's her birthday she's going to want some birthday sex or something."

"She might, and I'll give it to her. I fuck her all the time, but that don't mean shit to me because I make love to your mean ass." Damien grabbed Alex by the neck and pulled him to him. "Now that's what matters to me."

With nothing left to be said, Alex led Damien to his room. Since he'd been cleaning all day and could smell the bleach on himself, he changed his mind about the bedroom and led him to the bathroom instead. He flipped the shower on before undressing Damien then himself. Once they were both nude, they got beneath the flow of the warm water where they stayed for almost an hour.

When their shower was over, they were both tired and satisfied. The heat from the water had them both so exhausted that they fell asleep in Alex's room. Content with the moment, Alex snuggled up under Damien and got comfortable. By the time they woke up, it was going on four o'clock. Damien scrambled to his feet, trying to gather his clothing.

He was stumbling and falling all over himself trying to get dressed. "Damn. I'm late as fuck. We were supposed to have lunch at two."

Alex offered nothing because honestly he couldn't care less about it being her birthday or that they had lunch plans. He propped his head in his hand and watched Damien get himself back together.

"Why you ain't wake me up?"

"Why don't you just stay here? You claim this is where you want to be and that you love me and not her. Why do you care about her birthday?"

Damien looked at Alex with concerned eyes but continued dressing. Just like all the other times, he had come over, used Alex, and was about to go running back home to his fake life. Alex just shook his head and lay back on the pillow. That was one of the main reasons he'd made up his mind to stop dealing with Damien altogether. He always felt used afterward.

"Don't sit over there looking like that. You already know what's up."

Alex was so tired of hearing that same old line, but Damien was right. He did know what was up. His time with Damien; that shit was over. This would be the last day he allowed Damien to play him like he and his feelings didn't matter.

"You gon walk me to the door?"

Alex thought about saying no, but making Damien leave after he said what he had to say would probably be a lot easier if they were already at the door and not still in his bedroom. With one swift motion, Alex threw the covers back and got out of bed. He slid on the cotton shorts that were near his dresser and followed Damien to the door. When he was about to leave, Damien turned around and grabbed Alex's face.

Since he planned for this to be the last time he took it there with Damien, he allowed him to kiss him. Damien's kiss felt so good to Alex that it had his mind wondering about just one more time. Then reality hit, that was the same thing that had landed him right back in the spot he was in.

"Damien, don't come back. I'm done being used. Go be with your baby mama and leave me the fuck alone."

The look on Damien's face was priceless. Alex couldn't tell whether he was shocked, mad, or hurt, but whatever it was, it was showing. He stood stuck in Alex's doorway, unsure of what to say. He held his hands out by his sides as if asking what he'd done wrong, but none of that mattered. Alex was done explaining.

"Don't do this," Damien finally found his voice.

"I'm not doing anything. You are. You're doing this to yourself. You continue to come over here and play with my feelings like they don't mean anything and I'm tired. Whether or not my heart means something to you, it means something to me. I'm not about to keep letting you hurt my feelings over and over for nothing."

"I'm not trying to do that."

"Yes, you are, and I'm letting you, but not anymore. I'm done." Alex tried to close his door on the last part, but Damien's hand stopped it.

"You're serious?"

"As a heart attack."

"What do I have to do to make this right?" Damien pleaded.

"There's nothing you can do."

Damien took a step back into the house. "How do you know there's nothing I can do?"

"Because I know what I need, and it's not what you can offer at the moment."

"Just tell me."

"Leave your baby mama and be with me. Stop lying about who you are and let's just be together."

Damien shook his head and looked down at the floor. "Why do you always do this? You know I can't do that."

"My point exactly. Now excuse me." Alex pushed the center of Damien's chest until he was on the outside of his door and slammed it closed. It was so hard that he almost hadn't done it. The sad look on Damien's face was the same one he'd seen on too many other occasions to care about it now.

Alex made sure his door was locked before walking into his kitchen. He grabbed some oranges and a bottle of water before going to sit in the living room. He needed some time to think, and that little sex session with Damien had only made things that much deeper. He had been going back and forth about a lot of things regarding his life and his sexuality lately, and just like only Damien could, he'd come around and set him back all over again.

Alex was always so sure and positive that he would be able to turn his life around and try to do the right thing, but then his feelings for Damien or Troy would have him confused all over again. For him to love another man as much as he loved the two of them, the way he was living had to be right. Right? There was no way possible he could love another man like that and it be wrong. Even with his grandma preaching that for most of his life, he still hadn't put any real thought into it until lately.

He didn't know if it was because he was tired of being mistreated and used, or that he was really ready to make a change. He needed to figure whatever it was out so that he could get out of the terrible slump he'd been in. Alex laid his head back on his sofa and closed his eyes. He was in the middle of his prayer when his phone rang.

He could tell by the ringtone that it was either Summer or Rain. They were the only two with different tones. When he picked it up and saw Rain's name, he slid the green phone across the screen and put her on speakerphone.

"What's going on, Rain?"

"Nothing. What you doing?"

"Eating oranges and about to watch Grey's Anatomy."

"I need a favor."

"Damn, you don't beat around the bush at all, do you?"

He could hear Rain giggling before she said something else. "Not for real, but listen. I have a book conference coming up. I need you to go with me and do my hair and makeup. We'll only be out of town for that day."

"Yeah, I'll go. When is it?"

"Tomorrow."

"Now I should slap you. You know better than to wait this late to tell me something."

"I just found out too. Stop cutting up."

Alex could use the time out, so he didn't even try to cut up anymore. He simply agreed and told her that he would be ready to go tomorrow.

"Damien just left."

"For real? What happened?"

"Can you believe he came over here on his baby mama's birthday, fucked me, fell asleep, then hopped up and left my ass?"

"Dang, that's messed up."

Alex sighed. "It sure is. That's why I told him not to worry about me no more. I'm good. We don't have to be together no more. Not that we ever really were anyway."

"It'll be okay, Alex. I know you love Damien, but he's not the only man in the world. You'll find somebody else. You're too perfect not to."

Rain was as sweet as a piece of pie. She was always so positive and encouraging. That was one of the main reasons why he loved her so much. He could always count on her to make him feel better.

"You're the best sister in the world, Rain."

"So are you, Alex."

They laughed and talked for a few more minutes before ending their call. After talking to Rain he felt a little better about everything. Only time would tell whether he would continue getting better or falling back and getting a hundred times worse.

*****

The sun was shining as they rode down the expressway toward the building where Rain's book signing was. She and Alex had gotten up earlier that morning and prepared for everything. The signing was three hours away in Savannah, Georgia, and she was so excited. It was her first real outing since the fire, and she was so ready and excited to get back to herself.

Love had been having her holed up in his house, scared that something was going to happen the moment she stepped out. She'd allowed it for the first few weeks, but she was ready to get her life back. They still didn't know who the woman was that had attacked her, but she wasn't going to sit around afraid to live because of it.

It had taken some serious begging and some good oral sex to get him to change his mind about letting her attend. She probably still wouldn't have won the argument had she not brought up the fact that this was her livelihood and not some random trip. He got up and went to work every day, and she wanted to do the same thing. His face was balled into a scowl as she left the house that morning, but she was sure he would be okay soon enough.

"So what am I supposed to do while you're sitting around signing books?"

"Sit next to me. You can be my assistant for the day. Get me water and take pictures and stuff. Normally Summer does it, but you're here today, so it's your job."

"So, basically, I'm your bitch?"

Rain looked at him. "Basically, but you been that, so don't get brand new now."

"You play too much." Alex laughed as Rain turned into the parking lot and parked her car.

They both got out and began to gather the things that she would need to do her book signing and headed inside. Rain was actually glad that Alex was there because he was able to help her get everything set up and ready. Once they were pointed in the right direction, Rain noticed all of the other authors setting up their vending materials. She smiled and waved at a few people that were near her and continued on her way.

She wanted to hurry and get everything set up so that Alex could make sure her face was still beat. Being that it was two of them and she didn't have a lot of stuff, her table was up and together in no time. When they finished, she and Alex ran to the bathroom and made sure she was still put together. The pink silk shirt she was wearing was tucked neatly in the dark gray pencil skirt with the silver belt around her waist.

She wore silver jewelry and her hair was straight down with a few curls at the bottom. By the time they got back to her table, the doors were opening and the coordinator was walking around making sure everything and everyone was in their rightful places. Alex scooted his chair closer to hers and whispered in her ear.

"Okay, what I'm supposed to do, bitch? All these people coming in here."

Rain laughed at his nervousness. "Nothing, just sit here and look cute."

Alex had straightened his sew-in and parted it down the middle. His face was beat, as always, and he was dressed casually in a fitted button-up shirt and pants. She was almost positive that everyone would think he was a girl today. He looked so much like one, if she hadn't known him personally for so long, his gender would have gotten past her, too.

"Oh my God! I love your books." A tall, light-skinned girl walked to Rain's table and said.

And so it began. From that moment on, Rain was smiling, talking, and signing books. The signing was set to last for five hours, so she made herself comfortable and had fun doing what she loved the most. By the time it was over, she and Alex were both relieved. Her hand was tired and so were her cheeks. She had been smiling all day. Though her face was in pain, she was grateful. If it weren't for her readers, she wouldn't be where she was. She loved them just as much as she loved writing because they made it all possible.

She was walking out of the door with some of her stuff when she heard loud music coming from across the parking lot. Her head, along with everyone else's in the parking lot, looked to see where it was coming from. When Rain's eyes landed on Love's truck, she couldn't do nothing but smile.

"Now why your man got to be a nigga? He couldn't cut that damn music down?"

Rain shrugged. "I don't even know what he's doing here."

Alex pushed Rain's shoulder. "Don't try to act like you ain't happy. I can see it all over your face. You ready to see that nigga."

Rain couldn't even stop smiling because Alex was right. She was still smiling when Love's truck pulled up in front of her. The people around them were all standing around looking. Some were a little more discreet than others, but some were flat out staring. Rain couldn't blame them, given the scene Love had just made with all that loud music.

"Y'all make me sick," Alex mumbled, as he looked through Love's passenger side window.

Love was sitting behind the steering wheel smiling at Rain. He used one of his hands to push the locs hanging down, out of his face. Rain shivered at how sexy he was. He winked at her before getting out of his truck and coming around to where she was standing. He was dressed in a pair of black jeans with a red and white Red Sox baseball jersey and a pair of all black Jordan 12's. His hair was all down and his gold watch and necklace were shining beneath the sun.

His tall body moved with ease as he swaggered closer to her. Stopping in front of her, he bit his bottom lip while running one of his hands up the side of her face. He grabbed the back of her neck and pulled her head to his lips. He kissed her lips before moving to her forehead. Still standing there with an arm full of stuff, Rain almost melted.

When he pulled away, Love smiled down at her and grabbed the things from her hand. He turned around and placed them in his truck before doing the same thing with the items Alex was holding. When he was done, he turned around and leaned against his truck with his hands in his pockets. Rain was still standing on the sidewalk fighting back her smile.

"What are you doing here?"

"I came to get my books signed."

"Where they at?"

"In my truck." Love turned around and removed the books from his front seat.

Rain's smiled got bigger.

"Are you serious right now? You drove all the way down here to get books signed when she could have signed them before she left home this morning?" Alex looked at the smiling couple. "You know what? I don't even have the time for this." He smiled at both of them while shaking his head and walking to Rain's car.

When he was gone, Rain stepped closer to Love and grabbed his books. She pulled the pen from her pocket and opened the front cover of the first one. She walked closer to the truck and leaned on the back of it so she could write.

"Who shall I address this to?"

"Your number one fan."

With her head to the side and her eyes closed briefly, Rain tried her best to remember that they were in public, because if not, everyone in the parking lot was going to witness some serious porn action. Love's actions at the moment were such a turn on she could barely hold herself together. She looked over her shoulder at him and allowed her smile to make its appearance.

"You showing out today."

"How? I'm just here getting my books signed by my favorite author. I'm no different than everybody else."

"Oh, but you are." Rain walked to him and leaned against his chest. "They got their books signed, but you're making me fall in love."

He wrapped one arm loosely around the bottom of her back. "Am I? I thought you already were."

"I did, too. You just make me reconsider when you do things like this because I feel like I'm falling all over again."

He kissed her lips. "And to think you weren't going to give me a chance."

Rain's eyebrows furrowed because she hadn't given Love a hard time since the moment they'd met. "When?"

"That day we were out to eat and you were talking about that girl's shoes. I had to practically make you be my girlfriend."

Rain put her head down because she had totally forgotten about that. Clearly, she was the only one because Love sounded like he remembered it like it was yesterday, and it had been months.

"Well, I'm glad you did."

"Me too." He lowered his head and kissed her.

No one would ever guess that they were in public the way there were carrying on, kissing like they were at home. Love had his arms squeezed tightly around Rain while she had hers around him as well. The kiss felt like it lasted a lot longer than it really had, because before she knew it, he was pulling away.

With one hand, Love grabbed her wrist and pulled her to where her car was parked. Alex was already sitting in the passenger seat. He had the door open while he sat sideways in the seat talking on the phone. By the way his hand was moving and his face frowned, they could tell he was arguing with whoever he was talking to. As they got closer, he ended his call.

He stood up and looked at Love. "Your friend gets on my last nerve. You really need to tell that nigga to make up his mind. He can't be a real nigga still running around on the down low."

Love stopped in his tracks and looked at Alex in disbelief. "You're serious about that shit, huh?"

"Yes. I'm tired of playing with that nigga."

Love shook his head. "No, I meant about one of my niggas being gay? I don't give a fuck about your men problems."

Alex took a deep breath before rolling his eyes. "Next time you and Rain going through some shit, I'mma make sure I remind you that I don't give a fuck about your women problems. But moving on..." Alex flipped his hair over his shoulder. "Yes. I was serious as a fucking heart attack. That nigga is gay as hell. Telling me he loves me, crying, the whole nine."

"Man, you have to tell me who it is."

"Nah. I can't do that right now, but if he doesn't hurry up and do it or leave me the fuck alone, I got you."

"I need to know that shit now. I can't be kicking it with the nigga and he gay. He might be looking at me or something."

Alex smirked. "Nigga please. He likes his men a little softer. You're not his type."

"Yo, what the fuck, man. You wilding."

"He's really not." Rain interrupted.

Love looked at her. "So you know who it is?"

Rain looked away and smiled before nodding her head.

"Who is it?"

"No bitch. You better not tell this nigga." Alex looked at her across the car.

"I'm not. It's not my business to tell."

"You better be glad I trust you or I would make you break up with this nigga until the secret was out."

Love and Rain both looked at Alex with their faces filled with humor. "What you mean you'd make me break up with him. You can't do that."

"Oh, yes ma'am, I can." Alex placed his hands on his hips

"This hoe delusional." Rain turned around to Love and pulled the front of his jersey.

"Hell yeah." Love fixed her earring. "Y'all about to pull out now?"

"Yeah, we were. What you about to do?"

He shrugged. "I guess head back behind y'all."

Once they all agreed to leave, Love went back to his truck and they all left. Being that it was so late, the traffic that they'd run into earlier had disappeared and the drive home went by a lot faster than they'd expected. Rain was dropping Alex off at his house when he grabbed the steering wheel. Rain's whole car swerved.

"Alex, what the fuck?"

"Girl there goes Damien's car. Love's ass is still following us. He's going to swear I set him up. You can't stop right here. Go around to the back and let me figure something out."

Rain looked around the parking lot. She wasn't sure which car was Damien's so she was basically looking for no reason, because she didn't know what she was looking for. Her Mustang eased around the corner with Love's truck right behind it. He had only followed her because it was dark and he didn't want her out alone.

"Why is he here? I thought you broke up with him."

"I did. That nigga be acting like he can't take a hint. He's mad because I'm serious about not fucking with him, so he's acting crazy as hell."

"That's not safe, Alex. You may need to come back to Love's house with me."

Alex shook his head as Rain eased into a parking spot in the back of his building. "I ain't worried about Damien, Rain. He ain't that bad. Hell, I'm a nigga, too. If he wants to jump tough, then we can box up in that bitch."

Rain laughed at him before looking behind her to see where Love was. His truck was directly behind hers with the engine still running.

"So what you about to do?"

"I don't know because as soon as he sees me he's going to hop out because I told him that he couldn't come in."

"Why don't you just call him and tell him that Love is with me. I know he had to see that nigga's truck."

"I thought about that, but he acts so damn foolish sometimes he'll swear I did this shit on purpose, and I really don't feel like arguing tonight."

Rain and Alex sat in her car quiet for a minute, both trying to come up with ways around Love seeing Damien.

"How about I just leave my car here and have Dakota bring me back through here to get it after we go eat."

Alex looked at her. "You think he'll do it?"

Rain nodded.

"Okay, cool. Drive back to the front and park. I won't get out until y'all pull off. What you gon tell him?"

"Nothing. Love isn't that difficult. He's not going to ask that many questions." Rain drove back to the front of Alex's building with Love behind her. "I'll call you when I'm on my way." Rain grabbed her purse and got out of her car.

She could tell by the look on Love's face that he was trying to figure out what was going on, but she'd explain in a minute. She looked over her shoulder at Alex, who was still sitting in her car before opening the passenger door to Love's truck and getting in.

"What you doing?"

"I'mma just leave my car here. I was thinking we could go out to eat or something before we go home."

"Cool. Where you want to go?"

"Olive Garden." Rain could taste the chicken pasta in her mouth.

Love nodded and pulled out. He beeped the horn at Alex before pulling away. Rain wanted to turn around and look to see if Damien met Alex at her car, but she didn't want to draw too much attention from Love, so she kept her eyes forward. His hand on her leg made her look up. His eyes were still on the road.

Rain was happy that the restaurant wasn't crowded because she was starving and really didn't feel like waiting. Love held her hand as they followed the waitress to the back of the building. Once they were seated, they began looking through the menu. Rain already knew what she wanted, so she didn't need that much time.

"You're so fine, you make me want to cuss, Love."

He looked up from his menu and smiled.

"Whew! You so gotdamn fine it don't make no muthafucking sense." Rain shook her head. "You see what I'm saying? I can't stop cussing."

Love ran his hand down over his face. "Man, stop that shit, girl."

"Unless you can stop being so sexy, I can't do that."

Rain sat back in her seat and ran her hand through her hair. Love did the same, minus running his hand through his hair. He had it pulled back in a ponytail at the back of his neck. It was no longer down like it had been earlier. Rain's vibrating phone got both of their attention. When they saw the name, they both fell quiet for different reasons. Rain was happy. Love, on the other hand, she wasn't too sure about, but she'd worry about that later. She grabbed her phone from the table and answered it.

"Hello."

Chapter 4: The Pain of my Past

"Rain? Hey, it's Fallon. Are you busy?"

"Hey, boo. I had your number saved. I'm just having dinner. How are you? You feeling okay?"

Fallon's laugh was soft. "Yes, Rain, I'm fine. You asked me ten thousand questions in one breath."

Now it was Rain's turn to laugh. "I'm just so excited to hear from you. I honestly didn't think you would call."

"Neither did I, to be honest. I still don't know why I did."

"Because you wanted to talk to your new sister, that's why." Rain watched the discomfort in Love's movement as he sat across from her.

"You're too much girl... Umm Rain..." The phone got quiet for a minute. "I need to ask you something."

"What's up?"

The line was quiet again, but Rain could hear her breathing. She wanted to ask her what was going on again, but didn't want to rush her, so she just waited.

"Does my brother talk about me? Like does he ever say anything about when we were kids or does he wonder about my life now?"

"All the time. Not too much because I think it's hard for him, but he does."

Love grabbed Rain's hand and pulled it. She looked up at him but pressed her finger to his lips to silence him. She didn't want Fallon to get scared or nervous and hang up. Clearly, they were a sore spot for each other for whatever reason. He was shaking his head trying to tell her no, but she wasn't listening.

"When you talk to him can you please tell him that I'm sorry for the distance?"

"I sure can. Would you like to talk to him? I can have him call you."

"No. That's okay. If you can just tell him that, I'll be all right."

Rain could hear the pain and uncertainty in Fallon's voice. She wished so bad that she knew what had happened with them. It had to be something serious to cause them enough pain not to speak to one another, when the love clearly was still there.

"I'll be sure to do that... Fallon?"

"Yes?"

"Can I call you again tomorrow? You know, so we can hang out or something? I'm in desperate need of a manicure."

Fallon's voice held a smile because Rain could feel it through the phone. "Sure. Just call me in the morning."

"Will do. Talk to you later, sis."

They hung up the phone and Rain sat hers back on the table. She fidgeted around some, trying not to look at Love yet. She wasn't sure how he felt about her phone call yet. He hadn't appeared to be angry while she was on the phone, but she could definitely tell that it had bothered him. When she finally built up enough nerve to look at him, she was put right back into the same spot she'd been in while she'd been talking to Fallon.

Love's face was long with sorrow. His eyes were sagging in the corners and his head was cast down. He looked so lost that she could barely stand to look at him. Like comforting him was second nature to her, Rain got up to sit next to him. She reached for his hand and held it in hers, before laying her head on his shoulder.

"It's going to be okay, Dakota. She loves you. You want to know what she asked me on the phone?"

His voice sounded a bit harsh when he spoke. "What?"

"She wanted to know do you ask about her, or do you tell me about y'all childhood."

"Why does it matter? She doesn't care about me. She's made that clear as fuck."

"Kota, babe. Don't be like that."

Love played with the straw that was in his glass of water, but didn't say anything.

"You want to go home?" Rain looked up at him.

He nodded.

"You need to eat though."

"I'll just grab something on the way."

"What about your car?"

Rain had completely forgotten about her car. "I'll just get it tomorrow."

Love reached into his pocket and grabbed his wallet. He laid a twenty-dollar bill on the table to cover their drinks and the tips before ushering her from the booth. They held hands and exited the building. Rain tried to steal glances at him as they walked to the car. Even with him trying his best to hide it, she could tell it was bothering him terribly. The truck was quiet, and she had no desire to really talk, so she welcomed it.

She shot Alex a text letting him know what was up. After he told her that was fine, she called Summer. She hadn't talked to her all day.

"Damn, hey, big time. You getting too famous to talk to me now? I haven't talked to you all day."

Rain smiled at Summer's silliness. "Shut up, girl. It ain't even like that."

"I hate it for me when you really get famous. I'll probably never hear from you for real then."

"Stop your mess, girl. I just been running around and dealing with Alex and his foolishness."

"Oh, I know. He just called me. Where you at now?"

"Just leaving Olive Garden with Love; about to head to the house. What you doing?"

"Sitting at the studio with Jacorey grading papers."

"Oh, you just spend all your free time with him now, huh?"

"I got to spend time with somebody. Your busy ass don't have time for nobody but Love in the club."

"Um huh. I meant to tell you about your nasty self anyway. The way you and that nigga was all over my table the other night."

Summer laughed in embarrassment. Rain could hear it all in her voice. "Don't be embarrassed now. Drunk hoe."

"Mannnnnn, listen." Summer began. "You know what, hold on Rain. Let me call you back real quick."

"Now who's the busy one?"

"I ain't busy, I just can't really hear you."

"You good, boo. I'll just call you later."

They ended their call just as Love pulled up to Chick-Fil-A. He ordered Rain the same thing she always got before pulling around to the window to pay. She sat in her seat watching him handle things for her without her having to say anything. Even though it wasn't anything major, just food, she still appreciated him for the little things. She was still looking at him when he handed her the bag of food.

The drive to his house wasn't a long one, but it was long enough to give her time to think. She was tired of being in the dark about the issues with him and Fallon. He was going to tell her what was going on tonight. Silence encompassed them as they walked into the house. Rain had eaten all of her food in the car, so she went straight for the tub.

Love's bathroom was big and very nice, but it wasn't hers. She missed the feeling of being outside while she bathed. Her rocks and plants had done that for her, and now it was all gone. Before she allowed herself to get too far into her feelings, she undressed and submerged herself into the water. She'd pulled her hair up into a ponytail before undressing, so she was able to lay her head back against the tile without getting it wet.

"Dakota!" She yelled from the tub.

She heard movement before the bathroom door opened and he walked in. He was still fully dressed when he leaned against the sink and looked down into the tub at her.

"Get in with me,"

"I'm straight."

Rain raised one of her eyebrows at him. "That wasn't up for debate."

A lazy smile curved across his face as he began to unbutton his jersey. He undressed slowly, not really paying attention to the fact that he was turning her on. His sexy, chocolate skin ripped with cuts from his weekly gym routine. When he was in nothing but his briefs, Rain had to cross her legs and close her eyes.

"This baby is making me crazy," Rain said, more to herself than him.

Love's laughter caused her eyes to pop open. "I'm serious. The way I want you is getting ridiculous. It's almost like I can't control myself, and that's just plain ole embarrassing."

"No, it ain't. I'm your nigga. You supposed to want me." Love stepped behind her in the tub and slid down, before pulling her back to him. "I want you."

"I'm sure it's not like I want you."

"That's a fucking lie. Hell, I should be the one embarrassed. I ain't even pregnant, and I be with the shit any time you come around."

The laughter from the two of them resonated throughout the bathroom.

"Tell me what happened with you and Fallon, Dakota."

He sighed. "I really don't feel like getting into all of that."

"So?"

"Rain."

"Dakota."

He sighed again, but still didn't say anything.

"I don't have time to beg. It's either you tell me or you don't, the choice is yours. But I'm going to find out. Even if I have to get the information from Fallon."

"Don't do that."

"Well, tell me then."

"I don't like talking about it because it's little, but it turned into something bigger over time."

"I don't care. I still want to know."

Love was quiet and so was Rain. Neither one of them said anything. Rain wanted to give him space to talk, and he needed to see where he wanted to start. Ten minutes had passed before he said something, even though it wasn't anything that Rain had wanted to hear.

"I don't want to do this. It's the past. Let's leave it there."

Fed up with trying, Rain scooted away from him and began to clean her body. She was in such a rush to get away from him that she hadn't even washed twice like she normally did. She washed one time and hopped out. Covering her body with the large pink towel he'd bought for her, she made her exit. Rain slammed the door behind her. She wanted to make sure he knew that she was mad.

She was on her knees fumbling through the bags of clothes on the floor. She and Summer had gone shopping the other day for a few things that she needed. Everything was lost in the fire, including every stitch of clothing she'd ever owned, and it was very frustrating.

"Dakota! I need some fucking clothes," she yelled.

"We'll get you some."

Rain nearly jumped out of her skin. She'd thought he was still in the bathroom. She had no idea he was standing directly behind her. Rain's hand went to her chest as she took a deep calming breath.

"Why you in here yelling like you're crazy."

"Leave me alone."

Rain pulled the long, pink gown over her head and slid her panties up her body and walked around him before getting her scarf off of the dresser. Once her hair was tied up, she slid beneath the covers with her back to him and hit the lamp to turn the light off.

Love stood at the bottom of the bed watching her throw a tantrum. He wanted to laugh, but he already knew that was going to make her madder, and he didn't need that. The little attitude she had right then was good enough. Naked as the day he'd come into the world, Love slid behind her in the bed and tried to snuggle as close as he could to her.

He thought she was going to push him off of her, but surprisingly she didn't. She didn't say or do anything. She kept her back turned to him and pretended to be asleep. She might have thought she was getting somewhere with her attitude, but in reality she wasn't. He was in no mood to talk, anyway. Especially about the stuff she wanted to talk about. That was years ago, and he'd done everything he could to move past it.

It had taken him a long time to get to where he was. To the point where not speaking to or seeing the only family he had left on earth, no longer bothered him. In the beginning it would hurt so bad that he wished he had died that night with his parents, but he'd grown past that a long time ago and made it his business to never get to that spot again, not for anyone. Love rolled over on his back and closed his eyes. It felt like yesterday, when in reality it had been years.

Love's breathing was ragged as he stooped down beside the gas station. The gun he'd been given by Jude, the biggest drug dealer in the city, was secured tightly in his little fist. The weight of it had his hand sagging out of his jacket a little. He had been trying his hardest to keep it hidden so that he could do what he had to do, with no interruptions.

Tonight was the night he had been planning for months now. Never telling anyone of his plans. Not even Jude knew what he was about to do. As far as he knew, his gun was still tucked safely away in the bottom drawer of his desk. It was the day after Love's sixteenth birthday, and the day he'd promised to avenge his parents' death.

He had been doing his best to maintain the name his father had built, and today would solidify all of his hard work. In the back of his mind, he knew what he was about to do was wrong, but he didn't give a fuck. The images of his father and mother's dead bodies were still fresh in his mind and he had been waiting on this day for years.

Every morning when he woke up, every day he or his sister went without something, any time he needed to ask his father for something and couldn't, their faces would pop into his mind. Now was the time. His mind was made up, and the moment the two men exited the gas station it was over for them. It had been circulating around the hood who the robbers were that night.

Love kept a pretty low profile, playing it cool until he had to act out. He'd seen both men on too many occasions to count, and neither of them ever said anything. He didn't know if they thought he didn't remember them or what the case was, but nothing was ever done about it, until today. Today they would be forced to acknowledge his presence. Today would be the turning point for their family members.

He and Fallon's day had come long ago, and theirs was overdue. Love steadied his breathing before pulling the gun out and making sure the silencer was twisted on. The gold Camry was still parked near the dumpsters, so he was good. They couldn't stay in the store all night. With murder on his mind, Love crept over to the car, making sure no one saw him, and climbed into the backseat.

He'd followed them enough times to know their routines. They never locked any of the doors. It was dark and they were both pretty drunk due to their Friday night festivities, so he was sure they wouldn't see him. Love crouched down and pulled his hood over his head. Just as he was getting comfortable, he heard voices.

There was no need for him to look and see if it was them, because he already knew. Their voices were embedded into his memory. The gun slid out of his pocket slowly, still gripped tightly in his right hand. His heart was beating fast and his breathing was rapid, but it was show time. He couldn't waste any unnecessary time trying to get himself together.

When the car doors opened, they hopped in and started their drunken banter. The music was so loud he couldn't understand how they even heard anything the other was saying. Eight years had passed since the murder of his parents, and those two niggas looked every bit of it. Cleary, life had been beating the shit out of them. They looked bad as fuck. With no other thought in mind, Love sat up from the floor and raised his gun.

His movement caught their attention, but it was too late. The moment the first one turned around, he shot him in the face. The other one didn't stand a chance because before he could open the door and get out, the back of his head was splattered across the dashboard. Satisfied with his vengeance, Love crept out of the car as quietly as he'd gotten in, and ran back down the block.

He ducked into trees, running until he reached Jude's house. It was easy for him to sneak back inside without being noticed because of the party that was still going on. Jude's house was always jumping, which is why the perfect opportunity was presented that night. Love had wanted to wait until he was alone to get the men, but once he saw them at Jude's house, he couldn't. The moment they said they were heading to the store, he followed them out and handled his business.

Once the gun and silencer was clean and back where it needed to be, Love joined the party again. He moved around the room, silently nodding his head at the people he knew from around the way. The night went by in a blur after that. All he remembered from that night was getting sleepy and going back to their foster parent's house.

Mr. Steve and his wife, Coretta, had been their neighbors for as far back as they could remember, and had taken them in after their parent's deaths. They had tried all they could to keep him out of the streets, but Love had a mind of his own. He didn't do much, but he did enough to worry the old couple. He was nothing like Fallon. She was good, and did exactly what she was told.

Love was fresh out of the shower and lying down in his twin bed when he heard someone beating on the front door. They were beating so loud he knew without even seeing who it was that it had to be the police. He hadn't thought he would have gotten caught that fast, but so be it.

He was ready to do whatever time he had coming to him. His parents were worth it. Instead of trying to run or even go to the front door, Love stood up and got dressed in a pair of gray sweatpants and a white t-shirt. His white socks and Nike flip flops got him ready for his ride to jail.

"What did you do, Kota?" Fallon was sitting up in her bed looking at him.

"What I had to do. I love you." He walked over to Fallon and hugged her.

Although Fallon was three years older than him, he was much bigger than her. She got out of bed so that she could hug him better.

"I love you, too." Fallon's head was tucked into his arm when the door to their room opened.

Mr. Steve was standing there with a look of sadness on his face. "What did you do, boy?"

Still holding Fallon in his arms, Love looked at Mr. Steve and shook his head. "What I had to do. I love you and Mrs. Coretta, and I appreciate everything you've done for my sister and I. Don't worry about me and don't spend any money on lawyers. I'll be fine."

Love kissed Fallon's forehead before releasing her and walking to Mr. Steve and Mrs. Coretta. He hugged them both before walking to the door. When he opened it he placed his hands in the air and walked out onto the porch. Other neighbors stood around watching him get arrested.

He made eye contact with a few people, but nobody that mattered. He thought about his parents as he was being read his rights and pushed into the car. Love could see the tears in the eyes of Mrs. Coretta and Fallon as the car drove him away. He was in such a daze, he didn't even remember the ride to the station, only the interrogation room.

The white detective continuously questioned him about the armed robbery that had taken place at the local bakery. He knew what they were talking about because he had done that too, but he didn't understand what that had to do with him killing those two niggas earlier. The bakery had been something small he'd done last week for a few extra dollars and some bread.

Mr. Steve and Mrs. Coretta were going through hard times and food was scarce, so he'd taken it upon himself to rob the bakery and get some food. That wasn't even serious, in his opinion. He listened to the police question him and play the tape from the bakery for him. He admitted to that willingly, because he didn't care.

It was crazy to him how happy there were once he told them that it was him. They were high-fiving one another like they'd won something. He, on the other hand, had just begun to pull himself from the daze he was in long enough to realize he wasn't there for murder. He spent two years in the juvenile detention center and was never brought up on charges for the murders.

He would always laugh at the police department whenever he thought about how they just ruled him out as a suspect because they'd arrested him that night. They'd questioned him about it, but never charged him because they assumed he had been in jail at the time of the murders. How that never got past them was pure idiocy, but he would never speak on it.

The two years he spent in the juvenile detention center were enough for him. He'd met a nigga named Jacorey and they had become like brothers. Things for him were going okay. He had gotten his GED and everything. Mrs. Coretta and Mr. Steve would visit him every free chance they got, until Mr. Steve had a stroke and died. Mrs. Coretta didn't last too much longer after him. He assumed she had grieved herself to death.

After their passing, he was pretty much alone. Fallon hadn't come to see him since he'd been locked up, so he wasn't expecting to see her. She would write sometimes or send messages by their foster parents, but that was it. That's why the day he got called for visitation and she was waiting for him, he knew it had to be something serious. Now eighteen, and 6'4 Love strolled into the visitation room overshadowing everyone in there.

Fallon was taller and filled out into a grown woman. Her chocolate skin was smooth like his and her hazel eyes were the exact replica of his and his father's. She had her hair straight and hanging down around her neck and shoulders. When she looked up and finally saw him, her eyes watered.

"Dakota. Look at you." Her arms slid around his waist and his around her shoulders.

She hadn't gotten much taller, so she still came to his stomach. They hugged for a minute before she pulled away and took her seat again. Tears ran down her face as she stared at him.

"You have dreads now?"

Love grabbed one of the little twists he'd put in the other morning and smiled. "Something like that."

She nodded. "You look so handsome. Just like Daddy. Like, you look just like him."

"I know. The shit is crazy, right?"

"Yes. It's almost weird how much you look like him." Fallon looked around the waiting room at all of the other visitors before looking back at him. "I've been hearing some things."

Love already knew what she was getting at so he didn't say anything. Just waited to see what was coming next.

"Did you?"

Love knew what she asking, so he nodded his head up and down. Fallon's mouth dropped momentarily, before she closed it again. Her eyes glossed over as she grabbed his hands across the table.

"Dakota, I can't do this. I don't want to sit around and wait for someone to come and hurt you. I can't do it again. I'm moving away. My college is out of state, so I've decided to stay there and not come back here."

Love's chest sank in a little as he listened to her tell him that she was leaving him all alone in the world.

"You really doing this, Fallon?"

"Look at what you did, Dakota." She was full out in tears by then.

Love couldn't even take her anymore. Nor did he want her to bring attention to something that he'd gotten away with. With nothing but anger and disgust in his heart, he stood from the table and walked away. He could hear her yelling his name, but he refused to stop. She'd said all that she had to say, at least everything thing he cared to hear. From that day on, he hadn't seen or heard from Fallon until the day in the hospital.

Thinking about everything he had been through after getting out of juvenile hall still brought tears to his eyes, which was why he had no desire to talk about it with Rain. Not to mention how she might feel about him killing two people. He'd never told anyone that, except for Jacorey, and they hadn't talked about it anymore since the day he told him. Love was giving Rain such a hard time because he already knew that to tell her why he and Fallon weren't speaking would mean to tell her that entire story.

That was the one thing he didn't want to do, no matter how much she pushed. The only reason he'd even considered telling her was because he feared Fallon would tell her before he had the chance to do so. Love took a deep breath and released it before closing his eyes again with hopes of falling asleep. As much as he hated to admit it, he was probably going to tell her.

Chapter 5: Here When it Counts

Jacorey was stretched out on the small, leather sofa in the back of his studio listening to beats for his newest artist. His eyes were closed and he had headphones on. The black Beats that Summer had gotten him the other day had drowned everything in his background out. He wasn't expecting anybody else until later, so he wasn't worried about anyone disturbing him.

He moved his fingers to every tune and beat in the song as he bobbed his head along with it. He was in such a zone he almost didn't feel his phone vibrating. When he opened his eyes to grab it, he jumped. Almost falling from the couch. Summer was standing in front of him with her arms folded across her chest.

Jacorey removed the Beats from his head. "You scared the shit out of me."

"I should have robbed your ass. In here with these Beats on with the door unlocked."

"I ain't worried 'bout it."

"You should be. I could have been anybody."

"But you wasn't. What you doing off from work anyway?"

"See, you don't listen to nothing I say. I told you I had a dentist appointment today, so I just took a half day."

Jacorey nodded and held his arms out for her to hug him. "Show me some love, sexy chocolate."

Summer blushed and turned her nose up. "Nope."

"Oh. You acting like that today?" Jacorey got up from the couch.

Summer stuck her arm out in front of her. "Go 'head on, nih."

Jacorey paid her no attention and walked up on her until her back was pressed against the wall. He closed the space between them and leaned down so that his face was in front of hers. He kissed the tip of her nose and at the same time, he grabbed the side of her leg. He slid his hands from the side of her thigh to the back of it and grabbed a handful of her butt.

"That's all you do."

He shrugged. "I'm an ass man, and shawty you got hella ass. I have to touch it, look at it, or something."

"Whatever, crazy boy."

"Give me some love, Summer."

Summer began to blush again and kissed his lips. Jacorey squeezed her butt a little harder as she sucked on his tongue. When she finally released his lips, she pushed him out of her space and walked around him to sit down.

"What you got planned for the rest of the day since you off now?"

"Nothing, what's up?"

"I got a few meetings I want you to go to with me. One is at a restaurant in about thirty minutes, and the other is at a club later. There's an artist performing there that I'm supposed to go check out."

"Oh, that's cool. I'll roll with you."

Jacorey looked at the clock on the wall and walked over to turn off the lights. "We might as well head out now so we'll get there on time then."

Summer fixed her purse on her shoulder and followed him from the office. "You want to follow me to my house so I can drop my car off?"

"That's cool. I'll follow you."

Jacorey watched Summer switch to her car. "Gotdamn that ass be turning, girl."

Summer looked at him with a smile mixed with a frown on her face. "You need to just stop."

Jacorey laughed and hopped into his car. He waited until she was in and had pulled off then he followed. They took the interstate, so he switched lanes and pulled up next to her. He beeped his horn and sped off. Apparently, she caught his drift fast because she hit the gas and sped off right behind him.

She was switching lanes and passing cars just like he was. Even though he was in his car alone, he was laughing as if she could hear him. Summer was his type of girl. She was driving the shit out of her little car. He was so busy watching her in the rearview mirror that he hadn't even paid attention that she was now right up on him.

Her car swooped around his and charged directly in front of his as she cut him off. "Shit, Summer!" Jacorey yelled as if she could hear him.

When she took the exit to her house, she slowed down so they ended up at the light next to one another. When he pulled up, she already had her window down.

"Aye, gorgeous. You got a man?" Jacorey's voice carried from his car to hers.

"Nah. I'm single. You kind of cute too, you with somebody?"

Jacorey smiled and shook his head. "I got a lil mama I be kicking it with, but she cool."

"How cool?"

"Cool enough for me to smash you and her at the same time."

Summer rolled her eyes and drove off before saying anything. Jacorey laughed at her again then followed her the rest of the way to her house. When she pulled up, she threw her car into her parking space and got out. Instead of parking, he sat in his car and waited for her to join him.

Summer walked to his window and tapped the glass. "I need to run in my house real quick."

"Aight, but hurry your ass up."

Summer shot him a bird and took the stairs to her door. Jacorey sat in the car and tried to hold his urine, but was unable to. On top of that, he was thirsty. So he pulled his car into a spot and killed the engine. He hit the locks and took the stairs two at a time until he was at her door. His first instinct was to knock, but there was no real need to do so at the moment. She knew he was out there so she had to know it was him coming through the door.

When he first walked in he didn't see her, which was fine with him. All he wanted to do was use the bathroom anyway. He had been to her house a thousand times, so he knew where it was. Once he got to the top of the hallway, he could hear her on the phone. She wasn't talking loud, but loud enough for him to hear her.

"Nah, it's not that serious. We just be chilling sometimes... yeah, I like him, but he ain't really into titles so I'mma hold that down for a lil while."

Jacorey took a step further down the hall.

"I already told you if it doesn't work out with me and my friend then I'll holla at you, but I'm good for now."

When he'd heard enough Jacorey yelled her name. "Summer, where you at? I have to pee."

"I'm back here. Go ahead."

He had heard what she said, but he pretended not to, anyway. Instead of going to the bathroom, he continued to her room to see who she was on the phone with. When he rounded the corner she was still holding the phone between her ear and shoulder. She was standing near her bed in nothing but her shirt and her panties.

The pants that she had just taken off were in a pile on the floor. When she noticed him looking at her, she held up one finger, letting him know to give her a minute. He knew it was only because of the nigga she was on the phone with, so he went against the grain.

"How long you gone be?" He made sure to speak a little louder this time.

Summer looked at him and squinted. *Shut up.* She mouthed. Jacorey smiled and leaned against the dresser.

"Summer, come on."

"Josh, let me call you back a little later. Okay?"

She said a few more things before ending her call and throwing her phone on the bed. Before it could even hit the pillow good, she had walked over to him and punched him in the stomach.

"Don't you try that mess no more, Jacorey."

"What mess?"

"You heard me on the phone. So don't try to act like you didn't."

Jacorey grabbed her lightly by the front of her throat and pulled her to him. "Don't be talking to no other niggas then."

"But we're just friends though, remember?" Summer could barely get her words out of her mouth because of the pressure he was applying on her throat.

With her throat still in his hands, he pulled her head to his and kissed her mouth. "Our friend zone ain't like everybody else's, right?"

Summer's eyes rolled back in her head as she relaxed into his hand. "Right."

After hearing that, Jacorey released her throat and walked down her hallway. She stood stuck in the same spot for a moment, before he heard her moving again. He smiled at the wall as he relieved himself. He had Summer's head gone and she knew it. That's why she was fighting so hard against it.

He was cool with the friend zone thing, but clearly she wasn't. He could tell by the things that were said on the phone that she wanted more, but he didn't know if he was quite ready for that yet. In his heart he felt that he might be, but his dick was another story. He didn't know if it was ready to be tied down just yet. Summer had a lot of ass and some of the best pussy he'd ever had, but he still wasn't one hundred percent sold on the exclusive dating thing yet.

When he walked back into her room, Summer was jumping up and down, trying to pull a pair of jeans over her butt. He stood back, watching her wiggle and jump until she had forced every ounce of ass she had into her jeans.

"That don't make no gotdamn sense."

Summer looked at him. "What?"

"The way you had to stuff all that ass in them pants. It just don't make no gotdamn sense that somebody could be that damn thick." Jacorey laughed at himself and took a seat on the bed. "You almost got me sold, boo. Almost."

"Got you sold? Sold on what, nigga?"

"You being my girlfriend."

Now it was Summer's turn to laugh. "Who told you I wanted to be your girlfriend? Moving a little fast, aren't we?"

"Damn. It's like that?"

Summer nodded her head. "No titles, boo."

Summer was smiling, but he could tell she was serious. Just a few moments ago the joke was on her, now she'd completely flipped it on him. He wasn't sure how to take what she'd just said. All the time they'd been kicking it he assumed he had the upper hand, but Summer had just proved him wrong in a matter of seconds. On the inside he almost felt angry, but he had to check himself, because in reality he had no reason to be.

"Ready?" Summer stopped in front of him, dressed a bit more casual than she had been before.

The dark blue jeans and fitted white top matched nicely with her gold jewelry and long brown hair. Her face still held a small amount of makeup, but it wasn't too much. She had a small pink clutch in one hand and some open toe pink heels on her feet to match.

"Yeah." Jacorey wanted to tell her how nice she looked, but his pride wouldn't allow it.

He walked out before her and got into his car. She followed suit and hopped into the passenger side. They drove off in the direction of the restaurant. Summer kept trying to make conversation, but he wasn't really in the mood, so he barely said anything.

"Damn, lil yellow ass boy. What's wrong with you?"

"Ain't nothing wrong with me. I'm chilling." Attitude and sarcasm twisted together in his words.

"I can't tell. You sure are acting like something is wrong. A little too pissy for my liking."

"Nope."

Summer turned around in her seat and looked at him. "I know you don't call yourself got no lil attitude about me putting your ass in the friend zone?"

Jacorey turned his nose up at her and frowned his face. "Fuck no. I ain't stuntin' that shit. Hell, we are friends."

"Oh, hell. You cussing like that? Yeah, you mad." Summer laughed, and it pissed him off even more.

She always thought shit was funny. "You play too damn much. Your grown ass needs to grow up. You spending too much time at that school with those fucking kids. You getting too muthafuckin' childish."

Summer really laughed at that. "You big mad, ain't you baby boy?" She rubbed her hand down his face.

Jacorey moved his head to the side, but chose not to say anything.

"You want to be my boyfriend, Jacorey?"

He sucked his teeth and shook his head.

Summer smiled and grabbed the bottom of his face then shook it lightly. "Huh, Daddy? You want to be my boyfriend?"

He looked straight ahead and said nothing.

"You want to own all this sexy chocolate, don't you?"

Summer was taunting him and it was really getting on his nerves. He wanted to grab her throat and squeeze it, but the bad part about that was that he wanted to do that while she was riding on his dick. He shook his head, trying to get rid of every thought of her. He was happy as hell when he turned his car into the parking lot of the restaurant and turned it off.

Jacorey wasted no time getting out of the car, not even bothering to wait for her. He fought the smile on his face when he heard her behind him complaining. He didn't stop and allow her to catch up to him until he had made it inside the building and was waiting to be seated. Summer stopped next to him, but said nothing.

"Right this way, sir. Your party is already here."

They followed the hostess and were shown to a table with Ziggy and another man. Summer was shocked, but happy to see him.

"Ziggy!" Summer beamed, as she leaned over the table to hug him.

"What's good, ma? You doing all right?" He stood up midway and hugged her back.

That only heightened Jacorey's anger.

"I'm great. What are you doing here?"

Ziggy nodded toward a very stoic Jacorey. "My mans came through for me. I'm out of my old contract."

Summer took her seat. "That's awesome. I'm so happy for you."

"I'm sorry, I haven't had the pleasure. I'm Eddie Pen, Ziggy's agent, and you are?" The other man extended his hand toward Summer.

"I'm Summer."

"I take it you're Jacorey's girlfriend?"

Summer smiled bashfully, and shook her head. "No, we're jus—"

"Fuck no, she ain't my girlfriend." Jacorey's tone was laced with so much disgust that it almost made Summer feel uncomfortable.

Her face frowned instantly, as she turned to look at him. She was so caught off guard by his little outburst that she needed to look in his face. When he wouldn't look at her, she looked back at Ziggy and Eddie.

"If you two will excuse me. I only came in to speak." She stood back up and stuck her hand across the table to shake their hands.

"Ziggy, it was good to see you, love. Eddie, it was nice to meet you, as well."

Summer grabbed her purse from the table and walked away without looking back. She was halfway out of the door when she felt Jacorey grab her arm.

"Get your damn han—" Summer stopped when she realized it was Ziggy and not Jacorey. "Ziggy, I'm sorry."

"You good, ma? Why you bouncing?"

"Here you go with this lingo,"

Ziggy smiled. "My fault, ma. I just wanted to make sure you were straight. You looked a little pissed off when you left."

"I'm good. Just in a bit of a rush."

Ziggy stared at her like he knew she was lying, but he chose not to speak on it. "Well, let me walk you to your car."

"No need. I didn't drive. My sister is on her way to get me. Thank you, though."

"I'll wait out here with you then."

Summer pushed Ziggy's arm. "No. You go ahead in there and handle your business. Money first, Ziggy. I'll be cool."

"I ain't like that shit in there. That wasn't cool at all. We don't do no shit like that in my hood."

Summer smiled to keep the tears from coming. Jacorey had hurt her feelings more than anything. "He's just mad, but he'll be okay."

"Don't let it get to you, ma. It's niggas out here that would be glad to claim you as their own."

"I know." Summer said in a lower tone. "It's cool though. I really am okay, Ziggy. I'm a tough girl. I can handle a little talking."

Ziggy stepped closer to her. "Is that right?"

Summer pushed her hair from her face and laughed at him. "Ziggy, get your lil ass away from me."

He laughed with her before pinching her cheek. "Stay up, lil chocolate mama. He'll come around."

Summer nodded.

"Let me get my ass in here before I let you trick me out my money. I just wanted to make sure you were straight." Ziggy walked backward before going back into the building.

Summer pulled her phone from her purse and called Rain. She answered on the first ring.

"Hey, sissy,"

"Hey, skinny mini. Where you at?"

"Love's house. What's up?"

"I need you to come get me from the strip mall. I was at Cheddars with Jacorey, but that bastard pissed me off so I'm leaving."

Rain's laughter carried through the phone. "That's all you and him do. I swear. You sure you ready to go? Because you ain't about to do me like you did Alex. I drive all the way up there, you getting your ass in my car."

Summer snickered to herself and made a mental note to slap Alex for telling Rain. "Man, yeah. Come on. I'm walking down the strip mall looking lonely."

"Ain't nobody tell your ass to hop up talking about you leaving, knowing you ain't have no way home." Rain kept laughing. "Let me call Love and see where he's at. He was just at Hooters with some of the people he works with."

"Okay. Well, call me back because I can just walk over there. I might need to get me one of them firefighters anyway. Clearly they know how to fucking act. These stupid ass music industry ass niggas gon have me catching a case."

"Man, bye bitch." Rain hung up.

Summer was still smiling when she hung up her phone. Rain was so stupid. Since Hooters was right across the street from where she was, instead of continuing to walk, she stood where she was in front the furniture store until Rain called her back. She looked at the cars passing by, along with all of the people shopping.

There were people by themselves, people with children, and people with their significant others. Summer watched one girl and her man walking into Subway. He wasn't much to look at and neither was she, but they looked like they were in love. They were holding hands and everything. She wanted to roll her eyes, but not at them. She wanted to roll them at Jacorey until they rolled out of her head.

For him to be so cool, the nigga had the worst attitude in history. He was the main one screaming he wanted to just chill and he didn't like titles but was the first one to act out. She didn't understand him at all. Just before she fell off the deep end of her thoughts, her phone rang.

"What's up, Love in the club?"

"Aye, sis, what's up?"

"Tired of your stupid friend. Where you at? You still at Hooters?"

"Nah, not no more. I'm coming down the hill behind Cheddars now. Where you at?"

Summer looked around the parking lot until she saw his truck. She waved her arm in the air so that he could see her, and walked to the edge of the sidewalk.

"You see me?"

"This you standing over here looking like an orphan?"

Summer stopped smiling, and instead of waving her hand she held her middle finger in the air. Love was still laughing when he pulled his truck to a stop in front of her. He pushed the door open for her to get in.

"Man, get your ass in here and hang up."

Summer tapped her screen to make her phone hang up before getting in and getting situated. Love turned his music down and pulled away from the curb.

"Why you and Jacorey always showing y'all ass?"

Love was dressed in his dark blue firefighter jersey shorts and shirt with a pair of black boots. His hair was twisted back in one a long fishbone braid that touched the middle of his back. The smell of him flowed up Summer's nostrils, reminding her of his manly presence. He truly was a cool ass nigga. Even with him being as fine as he was, all she got from him was brother love. She could definitely understand why bitches like her sister would love him, but that was as far as that went.

Now that nigga, Jacorey, was a totally different story. He made every nerve ending in her body stand to attention. His tall light-skinned ass, with those sexy ass lips and eyes. Summer rolled her eyes up to the sky because she really hated the way he acted sometimes. It seemed like since meeting him, all she did was laugh or roll her eyes. They never had anything in the middle. That was their problem. They needed a medium.

"Man, that be that nigga."

"Let him tell it, it be your ass. It's probably both of y'all muthafuckas."

"No, for real, it be him. He tells me he ain't trying to be in a relationship, and he likes what we are and all that extra single nigga shit, but as soon as I agree with him or friend zone his ass he gets mad. I can't take Jacorey serious. He makes my damn head hurt." Summer looked out of the window.

"See what I'm saying? That's both of y'all. Why you be testing the nigga by bringing up the friend zone stuff?"

"I don't just bring it up, we be already talking about it."

"I feel you. Just give my boy some time. It's been a while. He ain't been exclusively fucking with nobody since I met him, and that's been well over five or six years."

"You only saying that because he's your friend."

"Nah. I'm saying that because it's the truth." Love pressed the button on the screen of his truck to answer his ringing phone. "What's going on, baby doll?"

"You got my sister?"

"Yeah, I got her orphan ass."

Summer punched Love in the arm. "Don't get the whooping I owe Jacorey's punk ass."

"Heyyy Summer." Rain sang.

"Hey bitch."

"You better be glad I like you. I don't let women ride with my man when I'm not around. Especially single women with butts bigger than mine."

Summer looked at Love and started laughing. "Girl, don't nobody want Love in the club's black ass."

"No bitch. Don't do that. My baby sexy as hell... see that's your problem, you keep running your ass behind all these light-skinned men. You better get on this dark-skinned train, boo. Those niggas is where it's at. Fine and got good dick. Whoooo! Dakota hurry up and come home baby. I need me some of you right now. Drop that smart mouth hoe off at home."

Love and Summer both were so busy laughing they couldn't even say anything back before she said something else.

"Nah, but for real, though, Summer. Where you finna go?"

"Home, I guess. I was supposed to go to another club with stupid tonight to look at some more rappers, but that shit ain't happening."

"Why, Summer? You gon stay mad that long?" Love asked her.

"Yeah. He hurt my feelings for real. You should have seen how he tried to flex on me in front of those people. You would have thought I was some dusty foot bitch from the hood."

"I'mma slap him when I see him."

"Yo pregnant ass ain't gon do shit," Love told Rain, making her laugh.

"It's cool, sis. I ain't worried about that. I'll call you when I get inside. We just pulled up at my house."

"K. Kota, hurry up and come home. I miss you."

"Miss you too, baby doll. I'm on the way."

"Can y'all lay off all the lovey dovey shit? I'm going through right now." Summer opened the door and jumped out.

"Just take your ass in the house. I shouldn't have even picked you up. When me and Rain was into it, you was stiff-arming my ass like hell." Love's smile made everything he said that much funnier.

"That's how it goes. Nothing personal. Appreciate you Dakota Love."

"You got it, Summer. I'll holla at my boy for you."

"Don't do that. I'm good."

She closed the door and waited for him to pull off, before she went in the house. Once she got in, she took her shoes off before unbuttoning her shirt and peeling her jeans off. Once she was comfortable in her panties and bra, she grabbed her ice cream from the freezer and made herself comfortable on her sofa.

The dark brown throw blanket that she normally had over the back of her sofa was now thrown across her legs, leaving the top part of her body exposed. Summer had scooted down and was deep into the movie *Brotherly Love* on Netflix when she heard her phone ringing. She looked around, trying to locate where it was. When she saw that it was on the dining room table, she made up her mind to just call whoever it was back.

She was in no mood to get up. Her couch was too comfortable and she wasn't really in the mood to be talking anyway. Her eyes had just gone back to her show when it rang again. Summer huffed as she stood from the sofa, almost tripping over her blanket and walked to her phone. When she saw Jacorey's number she had the mind to let it continue ringing.

"What?" she answered, with an attitude.

"Summer…" He sounded breathless.

She lost her attitude. "Jacorey? What's wrong with you? What you doing?'

"I'm outsi—"

Summer almost hadn't heard what he said because he'd said it so low. With nothing but her blanket wrapped around her, Summer took off running out of her apartment. When she saw Jacorey's car parked in the same visitor's spot that he always took, she ran to him. His window was down and he was laid back in his seat.

His eyes were closed and he was holding the side of his stomach. "It hurts, Summer time." He spoke through the pain.

The sweat covering his forehead and arms let her know that he was serious. He was breathing hard and his body was almost balled up in his seat.

"Can you move?"

He shook his head.

"You gon have to. I need to drive you. What did you eat?"

"Catfish and macaroni and cheese." He squinted tighter.

"You know better than that. That was too much grease." Summer leaned in the car so she could see his face. "Let me run upstairs and put on some clothes then we'll go to the hospital."

Jacorey shook his head. "Call the ambulance."

"Damn, bae, it's that bad?"

He nodded.

"Okay, I still have to go get my phone, but I'm coming right back, okay?"

He nodded.

Summer turned around, still holding her blanket, and ran back to her door. She ran straight to her room and grabbed a pair of black tights and her white PINK shirt. She combed her wrap back down and threw on her watch, then slipped on her black foams and grabbed her purse before running back into her living room.

Her cell phone and keys were back in her hand as she exited her home. She dialed 911 before locking her door, and told them her emergency as she walked to the car. Jacorey was in the same spot, clearly still in pain. He was balled up a little tighter in his seat with his head down. Summer took a seat next to him in the car. She squeezed as much of her as she could on the floor in front of his seat.

She rubbed the side of his face with one hand while placing her hand on top of the one he was holding his stomach with.

"The ambulance on the way. It's gon be okay in a minute." Summer looked away to keep herself from crying.

"Unnnn," Jacorey moaned and rocked back and forth subtly. "Summ—" He tried to call he name, but he was in too much pain.

She leaned her head on his arm and began to hum to him. "It'll be alright. I'm here." She ran her hand over his head. "We're going to the hospital."

Jacorey lay back in his seat, afraid to move. The pain was excruciating and Summer knew it. She had gotten on him the last time they went to the doctor about his gallbladder. The dietician had been very specific about what he was and wasn't supposed to eat. She didn't understand why he would eat something he knew was going to have him in pain.

Summer sat next to him, rubbing his head and stomach until she heard the sirens. The ambulance had just turned into her complex, so she stood up, wiped her tears, and walked to the edge of the parking lot so they could see her. The driver nodded his head when he saw her waving her arms. They pulled over and hopped out of the ambulance, quickly.

"What's going on with him, ma'am?"

"His gallbladder is acting up and he's in too much pain to move." Summer stood back so that the paramedic could squeeze in next to him.

"Sir, can you tell me what may have triggered this attack?"

"He just had lunch and it had too much cheese and grease. He's not supposed to be eating that kind of stuff."

The paramedic nodded as he touched Jacorey's knee. "Sir, do you think you can walk to the ambulance, or do you need us to put you on a stretcher?"

"Excuse me, but didn't I just tell you that he can't move? You need to get the stretcher, if you don't mind."

Jacorey threw his head back against the seat with his eyes closed, tightly.

"Yes, ma'am. I'll get it." The man stood to his feet and met the other paramedic at the back of the car with the stretcher.

"Summer." Jacorey reached for her.

Summer rushed to him and leaned inside the car so that she could hear him. "I'm right here."

"Help me up."

"You sure?"

He nodded.

Summer leaned down and wrapped both of her arms around his waist while he threw one of his arms around her neck. As soon as she tried to lift him up, he yelled.

"Oh, I'm sorry! I'm sorry, bae. I'm sorry." Summer apologized profusely. "Y'all come and get him, I don't want to hurt him."

"No," Jacorey told her. "Just help me. I can do it."

"You're too big, Jacorey, I can't lift you."

"Yes, you can. I'mma help you."

Summer didn't know why in the hell he wanted her to help him so bad, but she did it anyway. This time, she used a little more force and was able to help him out of the car. He was moaning quietly, but he did it anyway. As soon as he was on his feet, the paramedic rolled the stretcher behind him and helped him lie down.

Summer ran ahead so that she could get into the back of the truck and wait for him. It took both paramedics to load him onto the back before one jumped in and the other closed the doors. Summer kneeled next to him on the floor as they pulled off. His eyes were still closed and his body was balled up so close that his knees were touching his chest.

With him being so tall and big, he looked a little uncomfortable on the bed. Some of his body was hanging off in certain places, but he didn't seem to care, so neither did she. All she cared about was making sure he was all right. She grabbed his hand in hers and held it until they got to the hospital. They unloaded him quickly, and got him into the emergency room.

From there, things began to roll faster than she could keep up with, but she managed. He was in his own room with painkillers and an IV before she knew it. Wrapped in a sheet, Summer sat with her back pressed against the wall and her head propped up on her hand. Jacorey was lying in bed with his eyes closed. He looked to be sleeping, but she wasn't sure.

"Summer, you sleep?" His voice answered that question.

"Nah. How you feeling?"

"Like a bitch." He laughed, as she stood up from her chair.

She took a seat on the edge of the bed next to him so she could see his face. "Why you feel like a bitch?"

"Look at how I been acting today."

"You mean before or after the gallbladder attack? Because if it was before, I'm going to have to agree with you. You were definitely acting like a bitch. A lil bitty, stupid, spoiled ass bitch at that."

"Damn, you got a filthy mouth to be a teacher."

"So."

Jacorey turned over in the bed so that he was lying on his back. "I was talking about while my stomach was hurting, but I guess you right about the before part too."

"Yeah, you were fine during the attack. That's normal behavior for somebody in pain. Everything else was just uncalled for."

"I'm sorry, Summer time. I just get so caught up in my feelings sometimes. You forgive me?"

"Let me think about it."

"You must forgive me if you here."

Summer looked out of the door and into the hallway. "No, I don't. I'm just here because you needed somebody. That don't mean we're cool. If one of your other bitches would have come, I would be gone by now."

"Don't try to flex. I heard you calling me bae and shit when my stomach was fucked up. I couldn't say nothing then because I was hurting too bad, but I heard you."

Summer held her head down. "That didn't mean nothing, though. I just wanted to comfort you in your time of need."

"Um huh."

Summer got up from the bed and sat back in her chair. "You're too crazy. I can't deal with you. And you don't know how to take care of yourself. I really can't deal with you now."

"I can take care of myself."

Summer motioned her hand around the room. "I see. You take care of yourself so well you managed to end up in the hospital."

"I be forgetting what I can't have sometimes. If somebody wouldn't have been acting so crazy today, they would have been there to make sure I ain't eat the wrong shit."

"Well somebody wouldn't have left if another somebody wouldn't have been acting like a butthole."

Jacorey's hand ran over his face as he scooted himself back in the bed some more.

"That was your fault. You play too many games."

"How? We both agreed that we're just friends, but for some reason you only remember that when it's pertaining to you. Anytime it comes to me, that little bit right there just goes out of the window."

The room fell silent when he couldn't think of anything to say.

"I know I'm right, you ain't got to tell me."

"Man, whatever."

"Yeah, whatever. Either you good with just being my homie or you not. I'm straight either way. I just wish you would make up your mind and let me know what you choose because I'm not going to take too much more of your foolishness."

"I like what we have. No titles, we just doing our thing. I like it like that. It's less stress."

"So do I."

"Well, let's keep it the way it is."

"Will do." Summer looked at the door as the doctor came in. "Hi. How's everything with him?"

"Well, in order to stop the pain, we can do a minor surgery called a cholecystectomy. That's the simple removal of the gallbladder. This will prevent him from having any more attacks, but there is still a certain diet that he must maintain to avoid pain. I've noticed that the patient chooses not to follow his diet plan, so I'm going to ask you. Can you please make sure he's eating accordingly and following all necessary instructions?"

"Of course, I can. He's a little stubborn, but I can handle him." Summer looked at Jacorey out the side of her eye.

"That's my girl. Thank you," the older African doctor told her before looking at Jacorey. "Is this something that you would be interested in?"

"I'm interested in anything that will prevent me from feeling like I did today. I felt so bad I wanted to die."

Summer looked at him with concern on her face. "Don't say that."

"I'm serious, Summer time. That shit was hurting bad," He looked at the doctor. "Excuse my language."

He smiled. "It's quite all right, sir. I'll have one of my nurses come in to discuss things further with you before setting up an operation date."

Summer and Jacorey spoke their appreciation as he left. When he was gone, Summer stood up and pulled the curtains closed before sitting back down.

"Why you close the curtains?"

"I'm tired of those ugly ass nurses at that station. They keep looking in here like they lost something, so to keep from going to jail, I just closed the curtains."

A smile crossed Jacorey's face. "Why they can't look? I'm single."

Summer cut her eyes at him. "Don't fuck with me."

Laughter escaped his lips as he watched her. "You my fucking nigga, Summer time, for real. I love yo ass."

"I know you do."

"Your lil sexy, chocolate ass be wilding."

"You like it."

"Damn right." He scooted back some more in his bed and patted the empty spot beside him. "Come lay down with me. I know you got to be as sleepy as I am."

"Not with all these people coming in and out."

"I ain't thinking about them people, and you shouldn't either. Hell, it's a bed. We're supposed to lay in it."

Summer hesitated for another minute, but figured she might as well. After all, he was right. She was dog tired. The warm sheet they had given her when they first arrived was tossed to the floor as she climbed onto his bed. He pressed the button to lay the bed down flat as she scooted around, trying to get comfortable.

"We're too big for this bed."

Jacorey scooted down behind her. "No, we're not. See, we fit." He wrapped one arm around her waist and scooted as close to her as he could then hit the lights.

The room went completely dark, minus the lights from the monitors he was hooked up to. Summer couldn't remember anything past agreeing to get in the bed with him before her eyes closed. They were both fast asleep in a matter of minutes.

Chapter 6: Everything's Not what it Seems

"Did they say what room he was in?" Rain asked Love, once they got off of the elevator.

Jacorey had decided to go ahead and get his gallbladder removed, and the procedure had been that morning. Summer had called them a little less than an hour ago letting them know that he was out of surgery and in a room. Rain was glad that was over because Love had been acting a little weird all morning. Though he refused to admit it, she knew it was because of Jacorey's surgery. It was only natural. That was his best friend and he was worried about him.

"Yeah, it's 516," Love grabbed her hand, as they walked down the hallway. "Here it go right here." He knocked twice before pushing the door open.

Summer was stretched out on the let-out bed with the covers up to her face, and Jacorey was in his bed watching TV with the volume down. The light blue head scarf that was wrapped around Summer's head was the only thing you could see on her. The cover was over her face as well. Rain and Love walked in quietly and stood next to the bed.

"Damn, you look like shit, boy."

"Shhhh, nigga. She sleep." He nodded his head toward Summer. "I feel like shit, though."

"Boy, don't nobody care about Summer." Rain walked over to her and pulled the blanket from her face. "She needs to get her butt up anyway... Summer?" Rain called out to her.

She stirred a little before opening her eyes. They wandered from Rain, to Jacorey, then to Love, before falling back on Rain.

"Don't you see me sleep?"

"So? You have company now, so get up." Rain sat down on the empty space near Summer's legs.

"Girl, I been up all day and night. These people know they won't let you sleep. Every time you doze off good they're running their asses in here."

Rain and Love laughed at her grouchiness. She sounded so annoyed and it was hilarious to Rain because she could relate. The entire time she'd been in the hospital after the fire, people kept saying get some rest, but there was absolutely no way possible for her to do that with nurses and doctors coming in all hours of the night.

"My bad, baby. We just came to check on your sick-and-shut-in boyfriend before we went home."

"Well, if you came to check on me, why you talking to her?" Jacorey asked Rain, with a smirk on his face.

She was about to say something smart, but couldn't at the moment. The fact that Jacorey hadn't corrected her comment about him being Summer's boyfriend had her frozen for a second.

"You shushing us and shit as soon as we walked in the door." Love intervened.

"I just wanted Summer time to get some sleep. They been working her ass. They must think I'm incompetent or something. Every time they come in here they're asking her questions about me or explaining the aftercare to her. She might as well be the patient."

"Either that or your girlfriend." Rain looked at him.

His face was unmoving. No smiling, or frowning, just expressionless. "Might as well. That's how they're treating her. I know she has got to be tired."

"Well, we won't hold y'all, since y'all so tired. We just wanted to stop by for a minute."

"You ate today?" Summer rubbed Rain's stomach.

"Yeah. That's where we were just coming from. We're about to run by the store then head to the house now."

Summer nodded and Rain stood to her feet. She walked past the bed and tapped Jacorey's feet. "Aight then, Jacorey. I'll talk to you later. I'm glad everything went okay."

"Appreciate that, Rain. I'll holla at you later, Love."

Love walked to the bed and dapped him up. "Aight, my nigga. Summer, call me if y'all need anything."

She told him she would and waved as he closed the door. Back in the hallway, Love ushered Rain to the elevators with his hand at the small of her back.

"Which stores you want to go to?" he asked her.

She needed some more clothes, and he had promised to take her to get them. She'd gotten a few things to start off with once she got out of the hospital, but those were slowly dwindling.

"Let's go to the mall and Walmart because I need some socks, too."

"Cool."

Rain grabbed his hand when they stepped off the elevator. She was rounding the corner when her phone began to ring. It took her a minute to locate it since it was at the bottom of her purse, but she finally got it right when it stopped ringing. She was surprised to see Fallon's name when she pulled it out of her purse.

They'd set a date earlier to go get their toes done, but once the time came and Rain called her, she hadn't answered. Of course, that angered Love. He went off on a little rant for a while, telling her that it was time for her to let it go and that she could no longer be friends with Fallon. Which was why she was afraid to call her back right then.

She really wanted to talk to her so that they could build some type of relationship, but not at the risk of angering Love. He had his reasons for the way he felt, and although she didn't know them, she had to respect them. She didn't find too many people or too many things that he felt strongly about, so whatever it was with Fallon had to be serious. If he would stop being so secretive and just tell her, things would be a lot less complicated.

"Why you looking at me like that?" Love asked her.

Rain hadn't even noticed she was staring. When he called her out, she looked away and shook her head. "No reason."

"It's a reason. You probably just don't want to tell me."

"And you would be right."

"Why you keeping secrets?" Love placed his hand on her back again as they exited the building.

"Because that's what we do. We keep secrets from one another."

When Love's hand fell from her body, she turned to look at him. He was looking out over the parking lot, not bothering to acknowledge what she'd just said. It would have angered her had she not already known that's what he was going to do. It never failed. Whenever he got an attitude or she spoke of something he didn't want to talk about, he would get quiet and avoid eye contact.

The frigidness of his demeanor wasn't missed, nor was the small frown in his forehead. Maybe if she weren't so nosey or maybe had she cared about the situation with him and Fallon a little less, then she would try to make light of the situation, but none of that was the case. She wanted to know. Judging by the way Fallon had stood her up earlier, she wasn't dependable, so her best bet would clearly be to just pressure Love into telling her.

"Dakota, if you would just tell me then I wouldn't have to keep asking."

"If you would just leave it alone, you wouldn't have to keep asking, either."

"You make me so sick." Rain snatched open the door to the truck and got in.

Love followed suit, not offering any form of apology. With her arms crossed over her chest, Rain stared out of the window. They rode down the street in silence, with both of their feelings hanging in the balance. Rain, too angry to talk, and Love, too unbothered to make her. She could tell from the direction they were going in that he was still headed to the mall, but for some reason, she had no desire to go there anymore.

"Take me home."

"You so mad you don't want to go to the mall no more?"

"Just take me home, please."

She could tell by the way he sucked his teeth and blew out in frustration that he was getting irritated with her, but she was most definitely about to make that worse.

"I've been thinking. I think I want to get my own place again. Living with you is cool, but I like my own space."

"The fuck?" Love's nostrils began to flare. "You must really be trying to piss me off today."

"No. Actually, I'm not. I'm just telling you what I've been thinking."

"And you think you need your own house?"

"That's what I said."

"Cool. You want your own shit, then you can get your own shit. I don't have time for these little games you want to play. This shit is juvenile as fuck, and it's getting on my damn nerves."

"Well, if it's getting on your nerves so bad then you should be ready for me to leave." Rain looked out of the window.

She was sure she heard him mumble something about her being stupid, but she wasn't sure, so she chose not to respond. It wasn't long before he was pulling up at his house. Unlike he normally did, Love walked straight into the house. He didn't open the door for her or wait on her to get out. He was in his house and had disappeared from the front before she could even unbuckle her seatbelt.

Versus getting out and following him around to make sure he was all right, she sat in the truck and called Alex.

"What's going on, Rain?" His voice sounded a lot less chipper than it normally did.

"What's wrong with you?"

He was quiet for a few minutes then she could hear him sniffling.

"Alex, what is wrong with you?"

"I don't know Rain. I just don't know anymore. I don't know what to do with myself. I don't like feeling like this."

"How do you feel, boo?" Rain hated to hear him sounding so sad. That wasn't like him at all.

"I don't know how to describe it. Like I feel used, but then I feel inadequate, I don't know."

"Is it because of Damien?"

"Yes, he's most of it, but I just feel so incomplete. I feel like there's something missing."

"You want me to come get you?"

He sniffed again. "No. You just stay with Love in the club. I'll be fine." He cleared his throat. "What you was calling me for?"

Rain sighed. "You got problems of your own, you don't need to hear mine, too."

"Yes, I do. Tell me."

Rain went on to tell him about Love and Fallon and how neither of them would tell her about their problems. She expressed Love's attitude and the way he had been acting anytime she brought it up.

"Well, mind your damn business, Rain. That ain't got nothing to do with you, for real."

"I just want them to get back together, or at least talk."

"That's your problem, always trying to fix people. Some people like being broken, Rain. It's easier than doing the work to make things better. The shit they went through might be too deep to open. Hell, it may be some shit that'll have you looking at them differently, so you never know. Just fall back and leave the boy alone."

With a suck of her teeth, Rain displayed her annoyance for Alex's reasoning. Although what he said made plenty of sense, it wasn't what she wanted to hear, so she had an attitude.

"I don't care about you having no attitude, bitch. You called me."

"Well, I don't care about you feeling like you're missing something with your incomplete ass."

Alex burst out laughing, as did Rain. "You pregnant bitch."

"So, you're a gay bitch. So, what you saying?"

"That I love your baby acting ass."

"I know you do. I love you, too. I'll call you later. Maybe we can pop up at Summer's house and make her ass cook."

Alex snickered. "Okay. Just let me know."

They ended their call and Rain unbuckled her seatbelt. She opened the door and jumped out of the truck. Not bothering to rush up the sidewalk, Rain meandered, stopping to look at the flowers near his porch and his neighbors. She was at the front door and into the house when he walked past her. He didn't say anything as he walked to the kitchen.

"This is why I need my own house," Rain called out behind him.

"Well, get that shit then."

Rain rolled her eyes and went into the living room. She was making things worse, but she couldn't even help it. She didn't want to argue, but she couldn't help herself. Every time he came around, all she could think about was making him feel how she felt with him keeping secrets.

"What you sitting down for? You need to get that computer and look up some apartments so you can get your moody ass up out of here."

"Don't talk to me, you inconsiderate nigga."

"I ain't inconsiderate. I just ain't about to sit here and kiss your ass when you're acting up for no reason. If you want to leave, then leave. I'm not making you stay."

"Good."

He shrugged. "Good."

The TV popped on when he held the remote up and pressed the red button. He flipped through the channels and stopped on football. Rain sat, watching him ignore her with a frown on her face. She probably would have still been looking at him had her phone not began to ring. She held her hand up and noticed it was Fallon calling again.

"Hello."

"Hey, Rain." She coughed for a minute before trying her best to clear her throat. "Sorry about this morning, but I wasn't feeling well."

"It's okay. How are you feeling now?"

"Not too good, but better... just one of those days, you know?"

Rain's heart got heavy just listening to her. "I know, boo... trust me, I know."

"Are you busy right now?"

"Nope, not at all. What's going on?" Rain looked away when she saw Love look over at her.

"You think we could meet somewhere? I need to get out of the house."

"Sure, what time?"

"Well, I'm on the road now so I should be there in about twenty minutes."

Rain was confused. "Road from where?"

"Albany. I live in Albany."

Albany was a small town a little over an hour outside of Columbus. Rain had never been, but Summer used to go all the time when she was dating Chance, a high school teacher that she'd gone to school with. Their relationship hadn't lasted long, but she frequented Albany a lot when they were together.

"Oh wow, I didn't know that. I thought you lived here."

"I wish, but no."

Rain could tell by the way that she'd said she wish, that there was more to the story, but she'd worry about that later. Right now she would just go with the flow of things. She didn't want to say the wrong thing and have Fallon back out on her for the second time in one day.

"Oh, okay. Well, are you hungry? I could surely eat again."

"Not really. I just want to relax. You want to go to a park or something?"

A park? Really? Rain wasn't too thrilled, but clearly there was something going on with Fallon, so she agreed. Once Fallon told her which park they could meet at, they got off the phone. Rain scrolled up and down her phone pretending not to see Love looking at her.

"I know you see me looking at you."

She continued messing with her phone, pretending not to hear him.

"Rain."

"What?"

"Who was that?"

"None of your business, now bye." Rain got up from the sofa and hopped up the stairs.

If they were going to a park, she didn't need to be so dressed up. She kicked her sneakers off, before her jeans and shirt followed. She then redressed in a pair of cotton shorts and a tank top. She slid her feet into her cheetah print flip flops and walked back out.

Downstairs, she grabbed the keys to her car and her purse and headed for the door. She only stopped because Love had gotten up and was following her. She turned around to face him before he could say anything.

"Why are you following me?"

"Because you need to tell me where you're going."

"Apartment hunting."

His face frowned. "No, you ain't. Your ass is going to meet up with whatever nigga you was just on the phone with."

"Really, Dakota?"

"Don't really me, Rain. Tell me where the fuck you're going, or you're about to stay your ass right here."

"Nigga, please. I'm grown."

Love reached down and snatched her keys from her hand. "Now tell me where you're going."

"To the park, nigga. Now give me my keys back."

"With who?"

"Fallon."

Love's entire demeanor changed as he began shaking his head. "No, you ain't. You about to stay right here. I told you this morning to let that shit go. Ain't no way in the world you're about to meet her no damn where."

"You act like the girl is going to do something to me."

"She might. You don't know that damn girl. Hell, I don't even know her, and she's my sister. It's been almost ten years and I haven't seen or heard from her. You don't know what kind of shit she might be on."

Rain leaned back on one leg and crossed her arms over her chest. "Well, go with me then."

"Nope."

"Well, excuse me." Rain snatched her keys back from him and headed for the door.

He was right behind her. "You don't need to be going nowhere with her. We still don't even know who set your spot on fire. She might have done it, for all you know."

Rain spun around. "You should be ashamed of yourself. That girl didn't do that, and you know it."

"I don't know shit."

"Whatever." Rain walked away again.

"For real, Rain, stay here. How convenient was it for us to run into her after all this time, right after your spot caught fire?"

"She doesn't live here, Dakota. She lives out of town. She's driving here just to meet up with me." Tired of fighting, Rain walked toward him. "She sounds like a lot is on her mind. She may just need a friend."

A'ZAYLER

Love looked away so that she couldn't see the look in his eyes. Ever since they had split up, he had been worried about her. Whether or not she was safe. How was her life and what she may have had going on? So, for Rain to come out of her mouth with something may be wrong with her, it put him right back into a bad head space.

"Well, take someone with you. Where's Alex?"

"He's at home, but I'll call him and see."

"Call him now."

"Dakota, stop acting up and let me go see this girl."

His rigid body and hard expression displayed his discomfort with the situation, but he nodded anyway. Maybe he was being a little unreasonable.

"That's your sister. You may not have seen her in a while, but you know she's not what you're making her out to be. You're just really hurt by her, so you're talking out of anger."

He kissed her forehead and turned around. "Go, before I change my mind."

Rain hurried to her car and got in. She cranked up and pulled away from the curb before she could even buckle her seatbelt good. The park was on the other side of town from Love's house, so she had a while before she got there. At least twenty minutes, so she turned the music up and used the time to sort out of her thoughts.

After a scenic ride to the park she pulled along the curb and parked near the swings. She looked around to make sure she didn't see anything out of place before getting out. After Love had said all of those things he had her nervous that Fallon might actually have been a part of the attack on her life.

It wasn't until she heard Fallon's voice again that she changed her mind. She had called Rain ten minutes into her drive to let her know that her GPS was wrong and she'd gotten to the park faster than expected. Rain looked through the trees and watched Fallon sitting in the park for a few seconds before getting out.

She took the long winding sidewalk toward her. Fallon's head was facing forward, watching the children play. Her hair was different today than it had been in the hospital. Instead of it being down, she had it brushed up into a neat ball in the center of her head. The long, black maxi dress hugged her body, showing off all of her curves.

The hospital gown hadn't done her any favors. If Rain could tell while she was sitting down that she had a nice shape, she could only imagine what it looked like when she stood up.

"Heyyy, sister-in-law." Rain made her presence known.

Fallon's head turned and she smiled when she saw Rain. "Hey, honey."

Rain smiled back then made her way to the bench and sat down next to her. She hugged her before relaxing back and stretching her legs in front of her. "I didn't have you waiting long, did I?"

"Oh girl, no. I was good. Just watching these babies enjoy themselves."

There were so many kids in the park that Rain couldn't focus. Being that it was such a nice day outside, she understood the parents' decision to bring them. It made her even more excited than she already was about her and Love's new addition.

"Trying to get away from your brother. He can be such a pain in the butt sometimes."

Fallon laughed, lightly. "Tell me about it. He used to worry me so bad sometimes, I would forget he was my brother. I used to want to kill him."

"Well, let me the first to tell you, it's only gotten worse."

They shared a brief laugh before Rain turned sideways, facing Fallon.

"Tell me what's wrong with you. You sounded sad on the phone, and you look even sadder in person."

"Do I?" Fallon asked.

"You do."

"Well, darn. I need to do better. Can't be having the whole world in my business because I can't control my face."

"I'm not the whole world, I'm just Rain. You can tell me whatever you want. You could start by telling me why you and my boo don't speak, but I'll save that for later. Right now, just tell me what's going on with you."

Fallon sat back and looked out over the park. Her eyes held a faraway look in them like she was in deep thought. She looked around at nothing in particular, but her eyeballs were moving all over the place.

"You know what's funny, Rain? When you can look at another person and judge them and their lives. The things they might be doing, and how you assume they're going to turn out, when in reality, your shit is way more fucked up. Excuse my language."

"You're fine. I cuss all the time, and my sister and best friend are even worse."

Fallon's smile was weak. "My life is so fucked up right now. Like it's so bad, I get sick just thinking about it."

"What's wrong?"

"Well, for starters, I'm sick. Sick as hell, and I don't even care. My desire to live dwindles more and more by the day. I spend so much time at home alone that I've forgotten what it's like to have a life. In the beginning, I was so optimistic about my future, but it's like the more I think about it, the harder reality slaps me in the face. Some days I be so depressed I pray for God to just take me on to be with my parents. It's got to be better than where I am now." Fallon's eyes were sad, but she didn't cry.

It sounded as if she wanted to, but it didn't look like it. Her face was still as sad and withdrawn as it had been since Rain had gotten there, but her eyes were fine. They didn't mist or anything, which was a sign of strength to Rain. She knew what Fallon had going on, though she would never tell her that, and if it was her, she would be in tears.

"You know you don't have to be alone, Fallon. I'm here, your brother's here, I'll even share my sister and best friend with you. They aren't the nicest people, but they'll be nice to you, and they're funny. Both of them are extremely funny people. You'll have a good time with us."

Fallon looked over at Rain and smiled. "You're such a sweetie. How in the hell did Dakota's reckless ass get you?"

"Okay, first of all, boo, don't come for my man." Rain laughed first, with Fallon following. Rain was happy to see a genuine smile cross her face. "And second, he's actually not that reckless. He's pretty calm and quiet. I'm usually the loud one. He has to keep me calm on most occasions. I don't think you believe me when I tell you that you're missing out on something great. He's awesome. Oh my God!" Rain smiled, as she thought about Love.

"He has to be to have you smiling like that."

"I wish you could see for yourself. He's seriously the best man I've ever known. Minus my best friend, Alex, but he's really a girl, so he doesn't count."

Fallon hollered in amusement. "No, you didn't!"

"Girl, yes I did. You ain't see that nigga when we came into your room at the hospital? He's worse than my sister and I when it comes to girl shit. That nigga is the biggest diva I know, but he's a sweetheart. He will do anything he can for you. I love him like a sister."

Fallon laughed again before playfully pushing Rain's arm.

"I have to meet this Alex again. He seemed like he might be a class act when y'all came to my room."

"He is, girl. He is." Rain sat back and watched the children play as their laughter mellowed out.

The atmosphere around them calmed down and became quiet, minus the surrounding noise.

"I have AIDS," Fallon spoke in the same tone she'd been using.

"How long have you known?"

"For about six months now. I found out when I was getting my annual. Whenever I get my pap smear I try to handle everything at once, especially since my husband isn't the most faithful person in the world. To be for real, when the test came back I wasn't even surprised. In the back of my mind I knew something was off with me, I just didn't know what, until I found out."

"Damn, that's crazy."

"It is, ain't it?" Fallon looked at Rain. "You could be in a committed relationship doing everything you're supposed to be doing as a wife, and still end up getting fucked over."

"Nah, that's not crazy. That's very sad, actually."

Fallon nodded her head. "Yeah, it is."

"Just because you're sick doesn't mean you need to give up. You still have your whole life in front of you. You can't let that nigga take that from you. Take your medicine and you'll be fine."

"Sounds easy. I thought the same thing at first until I realized that I have nothing or no one. I feel so bad about the way I did my brother. I know in my heart that if I'd never done things the way that I did, that I would at least have him. Shit was just so stressful for me back then. I didn't know what to do. All I knew was that I didn't want to feel the same pain I felt when my parents died, and that's all it looked like Dakota would bring."

"It's not too late to change things. He would still be there for you."

This time when Fallon turned around her eyes were watering. "How do you know? I know he has to hate me."

"He actually really loves you. He doesn't talk about you that much, but when he does, I can still hear the pain. You two really need to talk, especially now. You need him."

"I don't know. My husband isn't too fond of me having a life outside of him. It's like he purposely keeps me locked away in the house. I don't know why. We used to do everything together, but once he started hanging out with these new niggas he's been acting funny. He doesn't like for me to do anything or talk to anybody."

Rain sucked her teeth. "Girl, please. I ain't worried about your lil man. Mine will beat his ass if you want him to."

Fallon smiled at Rain and shook her head. "How you gon tell me not to come for your man, but you over there plotting to get mine beat up?"

With a shrug of her shoulders, Rain dismissed Fallon's comment. "Because he sounds like a monster."

"Not all the time."

"Well, some of the time is enough reason for me. You want me to tell Dakota on him? You can come stay with us."

"No, Rain. That's sweet and I appreciate it, boo, but this is my life. I can handle it."

"Well you need to handle it then."

"How old are you, Rain?"

"Why?"

"Because I want to know. So, tell me."

"Twenty-four."

"How you trying to give me advice when I'm the oldest? I'm supposed to be telling you what's up, not the other way around." She playfully nudged Rain's shoulder with hers. "I thought you were a baby. Well, not necessarily a baby, but, at least, younger than Dakota and I. You have such a sweet and timid spirit."

"Thank you, I guess." Rain snickered. "How old are you?"

"Twenty-eight."

"Oh, okay. So you and Dakota aren't that far apart?"

Fallon shook her head.

"How long are you going to be in town?"

"I don't know. I was thinking just until I finished meeting with you. I needed to get out of that house, and since my husband is gone for the next two days, I had some free time."

"You should come to my sister's house with me tonight. Alex and I are going over there to chill for a little while. It's going to be fun."

"I don't know about all that, Rain."

"Man, Fallon, come on. You owe me from our cancelled pedicure date earlier."

Fallon looked away before nodding her head and agreeing to come. "Just for a little while because I have to get back down the road before it gets too late."

Rain clapped her hands in excitement. "Come on, you can follow me."

"Just text me the address and I'll put it in my GPS. I need to stop and grab some food from McDonalds or something real quick."

"No, you don't. Summer's cooking. And believe me when I tell you that heffa be throwing down."

"Okay. Send me the address anyway."

Rain looked at her skeptically. She thought for a minute that Fallon wasn't going to come, but she wouldn't pressure her. If she came then she came, if she didn't then that would be her loss. She texted Fallon the address before standing up and getting ready to head to her car. She turned back around to tell Fallon something when she saw her walking toward the park.

"Fallon, what you doing?"

She looked a little nervous. "I have to get my baby."

This was news to her. She had no idea that Fallon had a child. "Girl, you got a baby?"

Fallon nodded.

"Why you ain't tell me? I want to see."

Rain walked back toward the park and followed Fallon to the jungle gym. There were three little boys playing. They looked to be no older than five or six. Two were black and one was white, so she focused on the two little black boys. She was about to ask Fallon which one was hers until he looked up and the sun caught his face.

His irises disappeared and his little eyes appeared to be see-through. The rays from the sun shining on the light brown pupils made them hard to see. He was a dark-skinned boy with shoulder length dread locs and the cutest little mouth. From what Rain could see, he was relatively tall. He was dressed in a black and red Jordan outfit with some all black Jordan's. The top of his locs were pulled up into a ponytail with the rest hanging down.

"Time to go, Mommy?" He looked at Fallon.

"It sure is. Come on."

Fallon and Rain both screamed when he jumped from the top of the jungle gym. He landed on his feet and smiled up at Fallon. When he got close to her, he wrapped one of his arms around her waist and they turned around to walk toward Rain. They stopped when they got in front of her.

"Rain, this is my son, Jazz. Jazz, this is your uncle Dakota's girlfriend, Rain."

He stepped forward and held his hand out. Rain smiled before taking it. "Nice to meet you."

Rain swooned over him before looking up at Fallon. "Aww, he's so polite, Fallon."

"He better be. He knows I don't play."

"Mamaaa," he whined as he leaned his head into Fallon's side.

"He is so cute, and oh my God. You already know who he looks like, right?"

Fallon smiled the biggest she'd smiled since Rain had first seen her. "Don't even tell me. I already know. I tell him that every day."

"So, he knows who ummm..." Rain diverted her eyes away to give Fallon a hint without saying Dakota's whole name.

"Yes, he knows who he is. I tell him about my family all the time. I told him I would take him to meet them one day. I just didn't know when."

Rain was bubbling with happiness. She couldn't wait to take Jazz to meet Dakota. He was going to be so happy. He loved kids, so to have a nephew who looked exactly like him was about to make his day.

"You want to stop by Dakota's house before we go to my sister's?"

Fallon shook her head, quickly. "I'm not ready."

Rain pleaded with her eyes, but Fallon didn't look to be budging. "You'll never be ready. Now is the time."

Fallon looked away and said nothing else. Rain watched her as she shook her head subtly from side to side. It was clear that she was thinking about it, so Rain stuck her hand out toward Jazz and he took it.

"Come on, Fallon."

Fallon looked up at the two of them walking away and stared. She stood in place for a few minutes before making her feet move. She followed them to Rain's car. Once they stopped and Rain asked her where she was parked, she pointed to the dark purple Maxima two cars ahead of Rain's Mustang.

"Girl, that's my favorite color. I love Maximas."

"Don't try to get on my good side because you're forcing me to do this right now."

Rain twisted her mouth to the side. "Come on, Fallon. I promise it's not going to be that bad."

"Does he know where you are?"

Rain nodded.

"I'm sure he doesn't know I'm coming with you. Right?"

Rain nodded again. This time a little more hesitantly.

"When we get there, you go in first and let him know. If it's cool, then I'll get out. I'm not in good enough spirits to be getting condemned for the past at the moment."

"I feel you. I'll make sure he doesn't do that."

It took a little while longer to get Fallon completely on board before they were pulling out of the parking lot of the park. Rain's thoughts were all over the place. She didn't know whether to call Love and tell him what was about to go on, or if she should wait to get there and then tell him.

She was confused because she didn't know if he was going to tell her no, or was he going to be on board. His feelings regarding his sister were so hard to read that she couldn't even begin to think of what his reaction might be. She's tried calling both Summer and Alex to get their opinions, but neither of them had answered, so she had to figure it out on her own.

Rain spent so much time thinking of what to do that she'd cheated herself out of time to come up with a solution. Her Mustang was coming to a slow stop in the driveway of Dakota's home. The thought of sitting there until she figured something out crossed her mind, but she didn't have time for that right now. So, instead of acting like a kid, she put on her big girl panties and got out of the car.

Her first instinct was to walk right to the door, but she stopped in her tracks. She had an idea. Seeing Jazz would definitely make things easier. Fallon's driver side window rolled down as she approached.

"Do you mind if take Jazz in with me?"

"Rain…" Fallon dragged.

"I just know he's going to be so excited. We can use him as like an icebreaker or something."

"Go ahead." Fallon pressed the locks on her door. "You ready to meet your uncle Dakota, Jazz?"

"Oooh, yes Mommy! Yes!" He scrambled to get out of his seatbelt.

Rain and Fallon both looked at him and smiled. It was the cutest thing. He was so excited he could hardly get out.

"How old is he, Fallon?"

"Five, girl. He's just tall for his age. My daddy was tall like that."

"Well, so is Dakota."

Rain grabbed Jazz's hand and pulled him behind her toward the door. She walked slowly to the door before turning around to look at him. His smile gave her the comfort she needed about the entire situation. Rain stood back up, took a deep breath and opened the door.

Chapter 7: A Fresh Start

Love was standing in the kitchen with his back to the door when he heard the front door open. He had decided to make him and Rain some dinner, so he had shed his clothing and was in nothing but a pair of gym shorts and one of his old firefighter shirts. His locs hung down his back as he moved around the kitchen.

Things between he and Rain had been a little rocky due to the situation with his sister, so he wanted to do something nice for her. Anything that would take her mind off of wanting to know about his past. On top of that, there was no telling what Fallon had told her while they were out. All he could hope for was the best.

"Dakota," she called out to him.

She didn't sound mad, so he breathed a little easier. Maybe Fallon had been just as hard as him and hadn't told Rain anything.

"I'm in here, bae."

"Uh oh, you cooking now?"

He smiled and turned around to face her. She was standing in the door smiling at him. "You know I do my thing from time to time. Come on and sit down. It's almost ready."

"What you make?"

"Just some baked spaghetti and corn. Nothing for real. I washed that salad off that you had in the refrigerator, so we'll have that, too."

Rain nodded and looked around the kitchen.

"Why you still standing up. Come sit down." Love looked over his shoulder at her again.

"Okay, but I have someone that I want you to meet."

Love put the top to the pot back over the corn and turned around. He crossed his arms over his chest.

"Who, Rain?"

The annoyance in his voice was loud and clear. He could tell she'd picked up on it as well because she held her head to the side and looked at him with pleading eyes.

"Why do you have to be like that?"

"Just let me see whoever you have with you."

Rain looked behind her and into the hallway. She waved her hand and stepped back. Love's heart nearly stopped when the little boy stepped in front of her. He had his little hands tucked into his pockets as he leaned back against Rain. His eyes trailed up and down Love's body at the same time as Love looked at him.

The two of them stood facing one another, taking in the other's presence. Love opened his mouth to speak but didn't know what he wanted to say. He looked at the mini replica of himself then at Rain before looking back at the handsome little boy. When he finally gathered his bearings, he squatted down so that he was eye-level with the little boy. He looked up to Rain with the question, but all she offered was a smile.

"Hey lil man, what's your name?"

He smiled and stuck his hand out toward Love. "Jazz. Nice to meet you."

His generic greeting was the cutest thing to Rain. That was exactly how he'd greeted her.

Love looked up at Rain with wide eyes. He looked like he wanted to ask a question, but Jazz continued talking so he had to wait.

"My mommy told me she would bring me to meet you one day, but she never told me when. I'm glad it was today." He reached out and touched Love's dreads. "You have hair just like mine. Yours are just longer because you're bigger than me. Mine is just little because I'm only a kid."

"I've been growing mine for a long time, that's all."

"I know. My mommy told me. She told me I could have hair just like you so we could be twins."

"We already are. Has your mom ever told you that you look like me?"

Jazz smiled and nodded his head hard. "Yes. She says it all the time."

Love and Rain both laughed at his dramatics. It was clear that Fallon had drilled that into his head on a regular basis. The thing about it was why? She'd cut Love out of her life many years ago. So why on earth would she tell her son about him? That was such a mystery to him.

"So you know who I am?"

Jazz nodded her head. "Duh. You're my uncle, Dakota."

Love's face lit up from his smile. He grabbed Jazz from Rain's grasp and pulled him to him for a hug. Jazz laid his head on Dakota's shoulder and wrapped his arms around his neck. Dakota closed his eyes and savored the feeling. He hugged him as tight as he could, without hurting him, before releasing him and pushing him back some so he could see his face.

"How old are you, Jazz?"

Jazz held his hand up in Love's face. "Five."

"Did your mom ever tell you that you have the same name as your granddaddy?"

"Yes sir. She told me she named me after him because she loved him so much."

For the first time in years, Love felt as if he wanted to cry. The innocence in Jazz's voice was the softest part, but the words he said were what pushed him over the edge. He quickly wiped his eyes and pulled Jazz to him for another hug.

"Uncle Kota loved him too. So much. He would have loved you so much."

"Mommy says I'll meet him again one day when we all go to heaven."

Love stood up and leaned back against the counter so that he could look at Jazz fully. "Where's your mommy now?"

Jazz turned toward the door and pointed. "She's outside in the car."

Love looked from him to Rain. Rain looked uncomfortable and like she didn't know what to say. As she should, since she'd just set him up. The entire situation was weird to him because all of the hate he had harbored against his sister for so many years seemed to dissipate. He wasn't angry, nor was he afraid to see her again like he had been before.

"I'll go get her." Rain walked quickly away from the kitchen.

Once he heard the door slam shut, he looked down at Jazz again. "You hungry, man?"

"Yes." He rolled his eyes to the back of his head and slumped his shoulders, dramatically.

Love couldn't even stop his laughter. He was so tickled by Jazz's behavior. He was so innocent and reminded him so much of himself.

"Okay. Sit down."

Jazz found his way to one of the stools and sat down. "I'm ready. What did you cook?"

"Spaghetti and salad."

Jazz threw his arms into the air in victory. "Yes! That's my favorite. I love spaghetti and salad dressing the most."

"You're more like your uncle than I thought. Ranch is my favorite."

"Mine too. Even though Mommy never wants me to have any. It makes my stomach hurt."

"Well, Mommy's right. You don't need it."

The sound of the front door slamming brought about the jitters again. His heart felt jumpy and his hands shook a little. He could hear shuffling and even a little whispering. He kept his back facing the door to give him some time to settle his nerves. He took deep breaths as he prepared a small plate for Jazz.

"Hey, Dakota," Fallon's voice was quiet.

"What's going on?" He spoke without turning around.

"You not gon turn around and give me a hug or nothing?"

Love finished fixing Jazz' plate and turned around. He tried his best not to make eye contact when he set the food down. He turned right back around and grabbed a fork and placed it next to his plate before stopping his movement. He stood tall in the middle of the floor facing Rain and Fallon.

Looking at her face brought about painful memories, but it also brought about happy ones. She too was the exact replica of their father, minus the small parts of his mother that he could see in her. She was a lot bigger than the last time he'd seen her, but then again, who wouldn't be? It had been years since their last encounter.

"How've you been?" She smiled at him.

"Fine. You?"

"Terrible. Lonely. There's more, but I'll save that for later."

Love's eyes diverted away from her quickly, before looking over at Rain. She looked like she was begging him to be nice, so he tried his best to mellow out his mood.

"What's been up?"

"A lot. I miss you." She walked closer to him. "I'm sorry, Dakota."

He nodded his head. "It's cool. That's the past." He stepped back so that she couldn't touch him.

"Jazz, your uncle Dakota has this really big TV in the living room. You can watch TV while you eat if you want. You want to do that?" Rain walked to him and picked up his plate from the table.

"Ooooh yes!" He jumped from the table and grabbed the hand that Rain had stretched out to him.

Once they left the room, Love turned back around to face the stove. His back was to Fallon. He was trying his hardest not to be angry with her, but he couldn't hide it. Her being there took him right back to his last couple of days in juvie, and those were some of the worst moments of his life. He could still feel her presence behind him, so he took as long as he could to fix he and Rain's plates.

"You want some?"

"If you don't mind." Her voice was soft, almost making him feel bad about being so gruff. "Especially if it's as good as the spaghetti Mommy used to make."

Love smiled. "Nah, I don't think anything I make will ever be that good."

He spun around and handed her the plate he'd made for himself and gathered the one he'd made for Rain and set it on the table. Once Fallon had taken her seat, he handed her the basket of garlic bread and went back to make himself another plate. Once he'd done all that he could do to take up some more time, he sat down in front of her.

Neither of them said anything, just sat in silence. He could feel Fallon looking at him, but she wasn't saying anything either.

"So, you don't say your grace anymore?"

It had totally slipped Love's mind. With her right there like that, he wasn't thinking straight. It was so much going on in his head that he could hardly focus.

"Nah, I do."

"Well, you didn't just then. You just sat down and started eating."

Love looked at her once more before bowing his head and mumbling his grace. While his eyes were closed, he asked God to make their encounter a bit easier than it was at the moment before lifting his head and saying amen.

"Why are you so lonely and miserable and all that other shit you just said?"

Fallon held her fork in mid-air as his question caught her off guard. She stuffed the food in her mouth and looked down, and back up again. She chewed her food and swallowed as his eyes bore a hole into hers.

"Bad decisions, I guess."

"Like what?"

"Choosing the wrong man to marry for one."

"You're married?" Now he was the one caught off guard.

She nodded. "To Jazz' dad."

"Yo, Jazz, is a cool lil dude, sis. Handsome as a muthafucka just like his uncle."

Love could tell the atmosphere around them was still too tense for his line of questioning, so he chose to go a lighter route. He didn't want to offend her and have her running off before he could finish talking to her.

Fallon's smile was so much like his mom's he almost got sad. "He is. He's such an amazing little boy. He knows so much to be so young." Fallon's face was one that only a mother would have when speaking of her child. "Sometimes I have to stop and ask myself who's the parent."

"It's that bad, huh?"

"You have no idea. He keeps me going."

There it went. The happiness and joyful mood went right back to the damp one from before.

"Talk to me, Fallon." Love ate a fork full of salad and waited for her to let him in on what was happening with her.

She paused for a minute, still eating. He watched her fork move around her plate, pushing her food from one side to the other.

"It's like everything was all good until it got bad. That's weird, huh?" She looked at him and he nodded. "It's like there was absolutely nothing going wrong until it all started going wrong, if that makes sense. But after the ball began rolling, there was no stopping it. I met Jazz' dad my last year at Valdosta State. We clicked instantly. Even though he was nothing that I wanted, I fell for him right away, and fell hard as hell." Fallon paused when Rain walked in.

Rain patted her shoulder before looking around the table.

"It's on the counter." Love told her, referring to her plate of food.

"How you knew that's what I was looking for?"

He playfully tapped her butt, "Because I know you."

"Y'all so cute. Then here goes my miserable ass."

Rain and Love laughed at her until she began to laugh at herself as well. "Girl, shut up. You ain't miserable. You may not be as happy as us, but you ain't that miserable."

"Let you tell it." Fallon pushed the chair out for Rain to sit down.

Once she was comfortable in her chair and had said her grace, Fallon resumed her conversation with Love.

"Like I was saying, everything was good, then he got a new job and wanted me to come with him. I told him I wasn't going as his baby mama, so we got married. We were so happy the first few months in Albany, but then he started hanging out more and more with the people from his job; going places, not inviting me and shit, so I started getting curious. I started going through his shit checking for any and everything until I started finding stuff. After I figured out he was cheating, I contemplated leaving him, but I didn't have anything, just my baby and him. No family, no real place to go, so I stayed."

"You do know that's your fault, right?" Love stared at her.

"Yes, Dakota, I know."

"Okay." He went back to eating.

"I confronted him on the cheating and he denied it like I figured he would, so I just sucked it up and went on. He seemed to do a little better after that, but he eventually went back to his old ways. Before long, he was full-fledged neglecting Jazz and me. He would come home, shower, stay for a few hours, lay up, and be on his way. I got tired of that shit so I stopped having sex with the nigga altogether. Shit really went left then. I didn't care, though. That was his fault." Fallon rubbed her mouth as she looked around the kitchen. "One day I went to the doctor for my yearly checkup and my world changed for the worst." Fallon looked at Love, who was now done eating and was listening to her fully.

"I have AIDS, Dakota."

You would have thought it was his first time hearing it by the way he reacted. His head fell and he had to cover his face to keep the tears from falling. He took a deep breath and swallowed hard. The vomit in his throat was threatening to spill at any minute, and he needed to stop it. Rain touched his shoulder and he shook his head from side to side. He sniffed one long hard time before raising his head again and giving Fallon his attention.

"It's fine, Dakota. I've come to terms with it. At first, I was really depressed, but it doesn't really bother me anymore. All it did was show me how short life really is. I want Jazz to know you. I've always told him about you, Mommy, and Daddy, but I wanted him to meet you for real. So I made up my mind and said that I would bring him here to see you. I had packed all of our clothes and we left. I wasn't feeling at my best, but I came anyway because I had promised Jazz.

Our second night here I went to the ER because I was getting a cold. When they found out I had a slight case of pneumonia, they kept me in the hospital because of my disease. If it gets too bad it could be fatal, so they wanted to keep me until I got better."

"So that's why you were at the hospital here instead of Albany?" Rain asked.

"Yeah, and when I saw Dakota in the hallway, I was afraid and unprepared to talk to you, so I ran. I'm sorry, Kota. I didn't mean to run away like that, I was just really afraid of what you would think."

"This is so fucked up, Fallon." He sniffed again.

"I know... but when Rain came to my room and found me, I knew I had to act my age and make this shit right. Being scared was no longer an option."

"Where was Jazz while you were in the hospital?"

"With his aunt, Iesha. His father has a sister that lives here and she keeps him sometimes. She and her baby daddy have a son his age, so he goes with them a lot."

"You know, when you dipped out on me I was so fucking mad. I got into all kinds of trouble for months. I ended up having to do six more months because I wouldn't stop fighting. If it wasn't for my homeboy, Jacorey, I probably would have never seen the bigger picture."

"Our Jacorey?" Rain interrupted.

"Yeah. We were in juvie together."

The amazement in her voice displayed the genuine shock she felt. "Oh dang, I never knew that."

"I'm sorry. I just couldn't take it. After I found out about what you did, all I could think about was somebody coming back to do us like they did Mommy and Daddy. I couldn't handle it. I figured it would be much easier if I just left before it all went bad."

"What did you do, Dakota?" Rain set her fork down and looked at him.

Love knew when the words left Fallon's mouth that Rain was about to ask again. He looked around the room, trying to figure out how to tell her that he was a murderer. He needed to find the right explanation for ending the lives of two individuals. True enough they deserved it, and he didn't regret it one bit, but he still felt the need to cover up his actions. Bouncing his leg beneath the table and avoiding eye contact, Love tried his best to wait her out.

"Dakota."

So much for that, Love thought.

"You haven't told her?" Fallon looked between the two of them.

Love shook his head, subtly.

"Well, you need to. It's the right thing to do."

Love's head shot up. "I know like hell you ain't telling nobody what's right and wrong? Shit, somebody should have told your ass that shit years ago." He was tense and a bit afraid, and it was coming out more like anger than anything.

Though he was angry with Fallon still, he didn't mean to pop off on her that fast, and that harsh, either.

"You're right, and that's why I'm here. Keeping secrets never helps."

"You don't have to talk to her like that. Just tell me what's up." The tone of Rain's voice let him know that she was done playing.

He had strung her along long enough, and clearly that was over with now. Love could feel himself starting to sweat. Rain and Fallon were both looking at him and making his feelings even worse. As much as he wanted to keep it to himself, Love gave in and told. He explained everything that happened from the time his parents were killed, to the day he got out of the juvenile detention center.

Rain held her hand over her mouth, then her chest then rested them both in her lap. The look on her face didn't allow him into her thoughts, just gave a visual picture of her being upset. She rocked back and forth in her chair until he finished talking. When he was done, the room fell quiet. He did the best he could to relay the story in the easiest way, but unfortunately, that still didn't help.

"So you killed two people?" Rain needed to make sure she heard that right.

"Yes."

"And you've never been charged with their murders?"

"No. Questioned, but never charged."

Rain looked at Fallon. "So that's why you left and you two haven't spoken in years?"

Fallon nodded.

"Y'all need help. Like some serious professional help." Rain pushed her chair from the table and joined Jazz in the living room.

Fallon and Love sat at the table, not sure what was going to happen next. Fallon looked ever sadder than she had when she'd come in, so Love looked away. He now had his own problems to tend to. He didn't need to take on her burdens, too.

"I'm sorry."

"How many times you gon say that shit, Fallon? What's done is done. That shit is the past; just let it be."

"Not about that, I'm saying about this." She pointed toward the living room. "About making her mad with you."

Love shrugged as if it didn't bother him that Rain might be mad, when in reality, it did. "She'll be all right. She's been asking since we've been together and I never told her. Now she knows. She can do what she wants with it."

"That's how you feel?" Fallon raised her eyebrow.

"What else can I do? Y'all females don't care about a nigga's feelings. Y'all just do whatever the fuck y'all want to do and call it a day. So shit, it's whatever."

"You can't be like that, Dakota."

"Yes, I can, too. She shouldn't have asked. It's not like I can go back and change what I did, just like the past doesn't make me who I am today. She either gets with it or not. There ain't shit else I can do."

"So where do we go from here? I would really like it if we could fix what's left and possibly build a new relationship."

"It's all good, Fallon. It was fucked up how you left, but like I said, the past is the past, and it ain't gon change shit about who you are today. I want to spend time with you and Jazz, so whatever you want to do, I'm here for you. Y'all can even move up here with us if you want. I could help you find a spot and shit."

Fallon jumped from her chair and hugged him. It took a minute, but Love wrapped his arms around her and hugged her back. Although they both knew it was going to take some time, he was hopeful that everything would work out.

Chapter 8: Feelings for You

The noise of the vacuum sounded throughout the apartment as Summer moved around the living room with it. She had just brought Jacorey home earlier that day, and his spot was a mess. He had clothes, shoes, books, paper, anything you could think of, laying around his floor. There were dishes in the sink, empty food containers on the counters, and the trash was overflowing.

Summer shook her head at the large mess because it was just downright ridiculous. She could understand that he was single, but that was no excuse for his apartment to look the way it did. When she'd first volunteered to stay at his home with him, he'd declined, expressing how dirty it was, but she'd insisted.

Had she known it was this nasty she probably would have gone on about her business. She thought dirty meant overflowing laundry, pissy toilet seat, maybe even clothes on the floor, but what she got was much worse.

"You need your ass beat out the frame for the way you living." Summer moved his foot from the coffee table.

"I told you it was dirty. I be so busy sometimes that I just rush in and out."

"Nah, your single ass probably just be running from one hoe house to the next. It don't be no need to clean up if you ain't never here."

"You trying to start some shit, ain't you?"

Summer shook her head and flipped the vacuum off. She unplugged it before wrapping the cord back around the hooks. When she was finished, she rolled it over near the door and left it there. She had gone by her house to grab everything she would need to clean up before coming back.

"Don't be sitting all your shit over there like I'mma take it."

Summer looked over her shoulder at him. "Nigga, as nasty as this apartment is, you need to be trying to take something."

Jacorey sat up on the sofa. "I'm trying to take your goodies, but you acting all busy and shit."

"Did you not see your place when I walked in here? I *am* busy."

Jacorey looked around at the now spotless room. "Man, I ain't worried about that shit. As long as I had clean sheets on the bed then I'm good."

Summer turned her nose up at him. "Ewww, are you serious? That is so tacky."

He laughed so hard that she had to join in. Before long they were both in a full fit of laughter because of his silliness.

"Man, you play too much. Let me finish putting this stuff up then I'll start cooking." Summer opened the door and took all of her things back down to her car.

When she got back upstairs, she plugged in all of the plug-ins she'd brought with her before going into the kitchen. It had taken her nearly an hour and a half to wash all of his dishes and clean the microwave and refrigerator. It was sparkling clean now. Summer couldn't stand a nasty house.

That was the one and only reason that she had cleaned his entire house. Cleaning up after a nigga had never been her thing, especially if he probably had other women parading in and out, but if she was going to have to stay there, then it needed to be clean. She'd promised his doctor that she would stay for a while and help him get himself together, but there was no way that would have happened with the way his place was looking a few hours ago.

"What you making?" Jacorey walked around the corner and into the kitchen.

"Some baked fish and steamed rice with shrimp. Something that won't fuck with that raggedy ass stomach of yours."

Jacorey took a seat at the table. "You got all the jokes in the world don't you?"

"Not for real." Sumer pulled the food out and began preparing to cook.

KNOCK! KNOCK!

Someone knocking at his door had them both turning their heads. Summer raised her eyebrow at him. "You expecting somebody?"

"Hell nah." Jacorey stayed seated. "Let em' stay out there."

"Um huh. You only screaming let them stay out there because it's probably one of your bitches."

"If you care so much, go answer it." Jacorey made himself comfortable in the chair, letting her know he wasn't about to move.

Summer wanted to ignore it and act like she didn't care, but deep down she did. She wanted to see was it another bitch and if it was, if she was any competition for her. When the knocking continued, she and Jacorey sat at the table looking at her each other. Minutes later, his phone began to ring. He pulled it from his pocket and looked at the caller ID.

"That's Melody. Go see what she wants."

Summer switched from the kitchen and into the living room. She looked out of the peephole and saw a short, Asian looking girl. The fuck? Summer snatched the door open and realized the girl was actually black. She looked at little caught off guard by Summer's presence, but that didn't move Summer.

"Yes?" She looked the girl up and down.

She was standing on the doorstep with a bag of what looked to be fruit. "Is Jacorey here?"

"Yeah, he here. You must want to come in?" Summer knew that was a stupid question, but she felt like being petty.

"If you don't mind."

"Well come on, then." Summer stepped to the side and allowed the girl to walk in.

Summer turned around and walked back into the kitchen, offering nothing else. When she got into the kitchen, Jacorey was in the same spot.

"You have company."

Jacorey shook his head. "No, my nigga, you have company. You the one took your fast ass in there and opened the door."

"Don't play."

"I'm not." Jacorey picked up his phone and started talking. "What up Snapchat? Why I'm chilling with my homie and another bitch pull up?" After that, he stopped talking. She heard a beep then it started back again. "Let's see how this goes."

Summer turned around and tried to slap his phone out of his hand, but stopped when she noticed the girl had just stepped into the doorway.

"Hey, Jacorey." She waved.

"What's up, Mel? You good?"

"Yeah. I heard you were in the hospital. I just wanted to stop by and check on you."

Jacorey finally turned around in his chair and looked at her. When she smiled, so did he. Summer's blood boiled with that one notion. If that was bad, she really got mad when he stood up and hugged the girl.

"These for me?" He grabbed the bag of fruit from her hand.

"Yeah, I didn't know what you could and couldn't eat, so I figured this would be best."

"I appreciate that." He hugged her again, this time stopping to place a kiss on her cheek.

Oh, this lil light-skinned bastard.

Summer nodded her head to herself before she continued to fix dinner. Jacorey and his confused ass bitch that didn't know whether she wanted to be black or Asian stood in the doorway talking about all kinds of shit. Once Summer slid the fish into the oven and put the rice on the stove, she excused herself from the kitchen.

She thought maybe this would have gotten Jacorey's attention, but that nigga was really in the kitchen acting like she wasn't there. She had a trick for his ass, though. Her dinner would be done in less than twenty minutes, and soon as it was done, she was bouncing.

To kill time, she went into his room and got on her phone. She scrolled through Facebook, and Instagram before getting on Snapchat. She was hardly ever on any of her social media because too many of her students had one, but she was bored today. Summer stood in the mirror taking pictures of herself and replying to various comments from Facebook.

Twenty minutes zipped by and she could still hear Jacorey and his friend downstairs talking. She'd assumed they were still in the kitchen, but was surprised to see them sitting in the living room. She had to do everything in her power to bite her tongue and not say anything, but he was making it hard.

They hadn't known each other long, but Summer knew Jacorey, and he was doing that shit on purpose. He either wanted to make her mad, or get a reaction out of her by playing the friend card. Either way, she wasn't about to let him upset her. She quickly removed the food from its cooking places and placed them in Tupperware containers.

She washed her dishes, grabbed her purse from the table and threw it over her body. With her keys and phone in hand, she walked into the living room and threw her two fingers up.

"Deuces, best friend."

Jacorey hopped up from his spot beside Melody and met Summer at the door. "Where you going? I thought you were staying here tonight?"

"I was, but I got shit to do. I'll holla at you."

Summer went out the door with Jacorey right behind her. "What you got to do?"

"Take a bath and bust this pussy open for a real nigga." Summer hit the locks to her car.

"Don't get your ass kicked, Summer."

Summer opened her car door. "Boy, if you don't take your ass back in that house and leave me alone."

"You mad or something?"

"Mad? Why would I be mad? I've only been at your house cleaning and cooking for you to entertain your bitches. Why would I be mad?"

Jacorey smirked. "I thought you were cool."

"I am." Sarcasm was evident.

"Well stop wilding then and come back inside... she ain't nothing but a lil freak. We can smash her together if you want." He smiled and Summer had to squeeze the frame of her door to keep from slapping him.

"Bye, boy.

"Stop tripping, Summer time, you know you're my nigga."

"No, actually you're the one tripping, and I know I am that's why I'm trying to get to my house." Summer hopped in her car and cranked up.

Jacorey stood there, telling her to get out, but she closed the door and pulled away anyway. If he wanted to do this, then she would, too. See if he would have that same stupid smile on his face when the shoe was on the other foot.

Jacorey had a show for one of his artists at the club tonight and had asked her to come with him. She'd been all excited at first, but now that they were semi-beefing, she was really excited. She would show his ass. On her way home, she dialed Rain and Alex to see if they wanted to go with her. Rain said no, but Alex was game, as always.

She checked her clock and it was almost nine o'clock, so she had just enough time to get home and change clothes. She'd already bought a cute red romper that she hadn't worn anywhere yet, so that would be perfect. Picking her outfit out in her head was something she did on the regular because she was always late somewhere.

When she pulled into her complex, she hopped out and ran up the stairs as fast as she could. As soon as she was in her apartment with the door closed, her phone started ringing. When she saw Jacorey's name, she didn't even bother to answer it. He called back two more times, only to get sent to the voicemail, once again.

When ten o'clock rolled around, she and Alex were both dressed and headed out. Alex wore a tight black dress with his sew-in wand curled. His heels were just as high as Summer's. The red romper and black stilettos had her body on ten. She'd flat ironed a few curls into her wrap and threw on some jewelry.

Once Jacorey saw her tonight, he was going to be on his head to act right. Being that she hardly ever went out, her fresh face was new to the scene. With Alex in tow, she sashayed deeper into the club. Alex had been fucking with the bouncer for a while, so there was no such thing as waiting in line.

Summer looked around the club at all of the people as they made their way toward the VIP section. Jacorey had already told her his company was going to have it bought out just for them. It was close to the stage and far enough away from the crowd to party, but still have a good time.

"Ooh bitch, there go your man." Alex nodded his head toward the stage where Jacorey was standing.

He was dressed in all black as normal with a royal blue fitted cap on his head. His watch blinded everybody each time he flicked his wrist to the man he was talking to.

"His fine ass," Summer said, under her breath.

"You ain't never lied. You need to go ahead and lock that down, bitch."

"Oh, that's the plan. He wants to keep playing friend shit, and I'm good with that, as long as we're each other's only friend."

Alex nudged her elbow. "I know that's right. Let's go get us a drink."

They were walking toward the bar when Summer spotted Ziggy, or rather he spotted her. He was seated behind some of the ropes with a few other dudes Summer recognized from the studio. The cup in his hand raised toward her when they made eye contact. She waved and kept it moving.

They were at the bar ordering drinks when she felt a hand on her lower back. "What's good, ma?" Ziggy's northern accent took her there every time.

Summer turned around. "What's up, lil fine ass boy?"

He chuckled. "Yo, Princess, you bugging right now, ma."

"Did this lil nigga just call you Princess?" Alex asked, looking Ziggy up and down.

"Girl, yeah. He says I look like the girl from Crime Mob."

Alex snapped his finger. "Oooh, bitch you do."

Summer laughed because she knew Alex was going to agree.

"You looking jazzy as hell tonight, ma."

Summer blushed. "Thank you. You looking sexy yourself."

Summer heard Alex clearing his throat and looked up. Jacorey was storming their way and he did not look happy. He reached around Alex and grabbed her arm.

"Damn. Just knock me over then."

Jacorey ignored Alex and looked at Summer, totally disregarding Ziggy. "The fuck you ignoring my calls for?"

"Because I'm single and I can do that shit."

"I don't give a fuck about your black ass being single or muthafucking double. If I call, you need to be answering that shit. And what the fuck is up with you posting your ass all over the fucking computer."

Summer frowned as she watched Ziggy walk away. "What you acting up for? You are not my man."

Jacorey pulled Summer closer to him. "Don't try me in this fucking club. You got this little bitty shit on," Jacorey pulled at the bottom of her romper. "Taking pictures on the sink with your ass poking all out and shit for the whole Snapchat to see. Now you all in my fucking artist's face. You want your ass beat, don't you?"

Summer shook her head. "No, I just want to act like the single woman that I am."

"So, that's how you feel?" Jacorey's eyebrows were furrowed together.

"You the one said we're friends."

"How many times do I have to tell your ass our friend zone ain't like everybody else's?" Jacorey's voice carried a little louder than it had been a few seconds ago.

That one line had Summer ready to give in. This was her baby, no matter how hard they tried to fight it or dress it up. He was hers and she was feeling him like crazy. She twisted her mouth to the side, trying to stifle her smile.

"Speak up, bitch. How many times does he have to tell you?" Alex snapped his finger in Summer's face.

She smacked at his hand playfully. "Until he means it."

Jacorey's chest caved just a little as he released the breath he had been holding. "I do mean it, Summer time."

"I can't tell."

"Yes, you can. You know I'm fucking with you the long way. You just like to keep acting an ass on me."

"Because, Jacoreyyyyyyy ahhhh." She pouted.

He smiled and pushed her hair out of her face. With her hand in his, he backed up to the dance floor. Summer yelled to Alex she would be right back before following him. The remix to Chris Brown's "Back to Sleep" was playing as he spun her around so that her butt was pressed against him.

He wrapped his arms around the top of her shoulders as she danced. He leaned down to her ear.

"You know how many of my lil freaks is up in here right now? And I'm all over your ass."

Summer blushed. "I don't care about them."

"You shouldn't because I don't give a fuck about them. Only you, so stop acting so damn mean all the time."

"Stop playing with my feelings and I will."

"Oh shit. Big bad Summer has feelings?"

She nodded. "For you."

Jacorey tightened his grip around her shoulders and kissed her ear. "I got some for only you too, best friend." They enjoyed the rest of their night before going back to his house *together.*

Chapter 9: Blurred Lines

"So, you asked the nigga, no no no, let me correct myself, you begged that gotdamn boy to tell you what was going on, and when he does, you flip out?" Alex placed his hand on his hip and rolled his eyes toward the sky. "Summer, come hold me back before I punch this lil timid bitch."

Alex, Rain, Summer, and Fallon were all seated in the living room of Alex's apartment having drinks and pizza. Rain and Fallon had come over after a long day of shopping. Jazz had gone with Dakota to the fire department to give Fallon a break. After the long night they'd had before, Rain was in much need of a break herself. She'd thought spending time with her friends would help, but she should have known better. Alex' mouth was too much sometimes.

"Timid? Don't do me, bitch."

"Don't do you? Girl, bye. You're doing your own damn self. You've been asking this man forever to tell you what went on, and when he finally does, you acting like you can't take it. You should have left well enough alone with your nosey ass. You can't fix everything, Rain."

"Had I known he was going to tell me he killed those damn people, I would have never asked."

Summer looked at Rain. "I'mma have to side with Alex on this one. He avoided telling you for a reason. You should have known it wasn't no simple shit when it took him this long to tell you. Like Alex said, you can't fix everything, Rain. Some things are better left unsaid."

Alex walked into the kitchen and came back with the Pineapple Cîroc bottle. "She's too naive."

"No, I'm not."

"Yes, you are." Alex and Summer said, at the same time.

"Y'all, don't do her like that," Fallon said, from the floor.

Alex held his hand up in the air to stop Fallon from talking. "You just be quiet because you still in the hot seat your own damn self. You the same one left the boy when he needed you the most, so you can't say shit either."

"Poor Love in the club." Summer's voice held much sympathy.

"Ain't it? That poor boy. All these crazy ass women he's surrounded by. No wonder he loves Summer's ass so much. Y'all two bitches," Alex pointed to Rain and Fallon, "are trying to drive the damn boy crazy."

"Now why you have to say that? I'm still sensitive right now." Fallon looked down at her lap.

"Nah bitch, raise your head up. Ain't no feeling sorry for yourself. You did it, so man up. It's the past, he forgave you, so move on." Alex walked toward her. "Now hold your shot glass up."

Fallon smiled at him as he refilled her cup with the clear liquor.

"Don't mind my bestie, Fallon, he's harsh, but he means well."

"I'm not harsh. These hoes are grown." Alex poured himself and Summer another shot before turning around to Rain, who was holding her cup in the air, too. "What you got your cup up for?"

"Your mouth got me wanting to drink. Pour me up."

"Bitch you tried it. Wait a minute, I'll get you some juice." Alex walked back into his kitchen and came back with some cranberry juice. He filled Rain's shot glass up before taking a seat on the sofa next to her.

"Why she can't have no Cîroc?" Fallon questioned.

"Because she's preggy." Summer smiled at Rain.

Fallon's mouth fell open. "Here I am pouring all my secrets out to you, and you can't even tell me I'm finna be an auntie?"

"I wanted to wait until Love was ready to tell you. Sorry, boo."

"Um huh. You better be lucky I'm in a forgiving mood."

"I hope we have a little boy that looks just like Jazz."

Fallon smiled at the thought of her baby. "Me too."

"Look at y'all acting like y'all know each other and shit." Summer was on the other sofa with Fallon on the floor near the table. "That's sweet and all, but I have a question for the pregnant one." She pointed at Rain. "You ain't been acting all mad and stuff with him, have you?"

"Not really. I mean I know he can tell something is wrong with me, but I haven't been that bad."

"Yes, she has. He was talking to her this morning and she walked right out the door and didn't say nothing."

"Oh, you on their side now?" Rain looked at Fallon.

She laughed and blew Rain a kiss. "I'm sorry, boo, but you're lying."

"She gets on my nerves. She act like he gon kill her ass or something." Alex threw his shot back and reached for the bottle again.

"He might."

Summer drank her shot and slammed her head back into Alex's soft sofa. "You can't be serious right now. You can't possibly think the same nigga that saved your ass from a burning house less than a month ago, will kill you today?" Summer rolled her eyes and poured herself another shot. "Slap her for me, Alex."

"Gladly." Alex's hand swiftly landed across the side of Rain's face.

He laughed when she punched him in the arm. "Slap me again, gay ass boy."

"Oh hell, Summer, she calling names. That bitch getting mad."

"Good. Now she sees how Love feels."

Fallon held her cup up for Alex to pour her another shot. "So that's what y'all call him? Love?"

The three of them all told her yes in different forms.

"That's cool." She drank her shot. "So when did he save you, Rain?"

"A few weeks ago. Somebody has been stalking me, leaving random notes on my car and stuff, and they finally got irritated enough to break in, I guess. Kicked in my window, nearly stomped my ass to death, and set my house on fire. If your brother hadn't come, I probably would have died."

"Oh yeahhh, you told me that while we were in the hospital."

Rain nodded.

"My brother is really not a bad person. He was just traumatized. He watched all of that happen." Fallon's eyes watered. "You know something, he's always been a fan of burning houses because he ran back into our burning home trying to save our parents. He was too small to move them and ended up passing out. The firefighters brought him back out."

"He told me that," Rain said, quietly.

Alex hit her upside her head. "And you still doubting the boy enough to be mad about some shit he did when he was a child?"

"Leave me alone, Alex."

"Or what? I'm not Love in the club."

"Summer, get him." Rain whined.

Alex looked at how pitiful Rain was acting and decided to ease up on her a little. "Okay, I'll chill. I'm just trying to tell you, Rain. You and Love in the club have been through enough. Don't bring up no more unnecessary issues. That's the past. He's been a murderer all this time and you didn't know it, so just leave it alone. Be happy you got a man that wants you."

"Amen to that." Fallon held up her cup and Alex and Summer touched it with theirs.

"How's Jacorey, Miss Fast Ass?" Alex wanted to change the subject before they got into his life.

He knew Rain like the back of his hand, and the ending of his last statement was more than likely going to draw some sort of sympathy or conversation from her. Normally he wouldn't mind talking about it with them, but things were different at the moment. Fallon seemed cool and all, but he didn't know her or trust her enough to be talking about his business, especially with Damien being on the down low. He wouldn't put out his business like that by being careless.

Summer being the smart girl that she was, winked at him and picked up the conversation. "He's cool. Still in a little bit of pain and whining like a baby, but other than that, he's good. It's going to take him some time to get his eating under control, but once he does that he should be all right. He just don't like to listen. He's like a little bitty child. As soon as I leave, he's sneaking to eat something he knows he can't have." Summer shook her head. "I keep trying to tell that fool, it's not me that he's hurting. Stupid ass." Summer's laughter was giddy and full of happiness.

"So you in love or nah?" Fallon asked.

"She is, and the crazy thing about it, Fallon, they love to act like they're best friends. Ain't that so childish?"

"Oh my God, yes. Y'all too old for that, Summer. Stake your claim, boo."

"Jacorey knows where it's good at. I ain't worried. The only reason I can't take him serious is because he does stupid shit. Like yesterday, some lil crossed-eyed hoe came over there talking about she heard he was in the hospital and wanted to check on him... like bitch... I know you see me in here?" Summer told them with her eyebrows raised.

"Then this hoe drags me off to the club to help make him mad. It ended up working though because they were damn near inseparable the rest of the night. Talking about bitches hating? Baby, let me tell you, they were big mad with Summer's ass." Alex was ready to tell the juice.

Summer went on to explain what happened. Of course, all of them had their share of comments and advice. Most of it was encouragement and playful banter.

"I ain't worried. That nigga knows what's up. He wants to play this friend role, then I'm with it. It'll happen eventually."

Alex slapped fives with her. "That's my girl. Get his ass, best friend."

They were all laughing when Fallon interrupted.

"Hold on, this the same Jacorey that was in jail with Dakota, Rain?"

"Yep."

"Aww, that's so cute."

"Dang, Alex, all you have to do is find you one out the crew, and y'all will have the whole team locked down."

Alex, Rain, and Summer all laughed amongst themselves. "Trust me, boo. I got that covered."

Fallon's eyes got large and her mouth fell open. "You lying."

"No ma'am, I am not."

"Scandalous ass niggas."

Alex agreed with her and made a few more jokes before that conversation died down. They all laughed and joked well into the night. The only reason they'd begun to disperse was because their men had started calling. First, it was Love, then Jacorey, then Fallon's husband. He wasn't too happy about all of the noise she had going on in the background, so he ended up hanging up in her face.

Jacorey and Love, on the other hand, had called back to back until their women left. Alex walked them all out to the car before going back up to his house. He was drunk and lonely, and all he wanted to do was go to bed. If he and the girls hadn't made such a mess, he probably would have, but he wasn't that type of person. He could never go to bed and leave his apartment dirty. He gathered all the food and trash first, followed by the drinks and cups.

He did the best he could with his head spinning. Thankfully, it didn't take long, and he was headed to his shower before he knew it. With his shower cap on, Alex stood with his back to the water and scrolled on his phone. He had been on Facebook first, then Snapchat. He was in the middle of watching his friend, Connie's story when Troy's name popped up on his screen.

"What the hell?" he mumbled to himself.

Troy hadn't reached out to him since the day that he'd left his home in a rage. He briefly wondered what he could want before answering.

"Hey Troy, what's going on?" Alex tried to sound as calm as possible.

"Nothing, just thinking about you. How you been?" His voice was lazy like he was lying in bed or something.

"Okay, I guess. Just trying to sort some things out. You doing okay?"

"Good as I can be... I miss you, though."

Alex was quiet because he didn't know what to say. He had missed him too, more that he'd thought he would initially, but he didn't want to seem desperate.

"I take your silence as you've been missing me, too?" Troy's chuckle was low and sexy as hell to Alex.

"You always did know me."

"Still do."

"What made you think about me?"

"It's just another day. That's all it takes."

Alex nearly melted into the wall. Troy was the sweetest thing in the world to him. The fact that he'd been that way since the day Alex had met him let him know that he was telling the truth. Everything he was saying was really how he felt.

"You alone? Or do you have company?" Troy interrupted his thoughts.

"I'm alone."

"Can I come over?"

"You really want to?"

Troy's breathing was all Alex could hear for a minute. "If you want me to."

"I do."

"On the way." Troy hung up the phone.

Alex smiled to himself and tossed his phone out of the shower door. It hit the dark blue rug face down. When the door closed back, Alex bathed quickly and rinsed off. Once he finished, he dried off before wrapping his towel around his waist and running to his room. He put lotion on his body and slid into his pajamas, then brushed his weave and ran back into the bathroom. He hurried to wash his face and brush his teeth.

Being that he was still very drunk, he had to focus a little harder to complete all the tasks. When he finished, he sprayed on some body spray and walked around his house, making sure everything was clean. Before going back to his room, he lit some candles and sprayed some air freshener around his kitchen and living room.

Back in his room, it dawned on him that he might need to change his sheets. He hadn't had company in a while, but he didn't want to take any chances. Troy hadn't said anything sexually suggestive, but he wanted to be sure anyways. There had been many nights where the two of them chilled with nothing happening other than laughter and jokes, but tonight might be different.

He replaced the black sheets on his bed with some light blue ones and remade the bed. He stuffed his dirty linen into the bottom of his hamper in the laundry room and went back to his bed. Troy was so nosey and extra attentive. The moment he spotted the dirty sheets he would assume the worst, and Alex wasn't really in the mood for anything like that.

The TV was on Law and Order as he snuggled beneath his covers waiting. He tried to keep his eyes open, but the liquor and the long day he'd had made that nearly impossible. Before he could stop himself, he'd fallen asleep. He probably would have still been asleep had he not felt a hand rubbing up and down his back, softly.

He jumped and grabbed his chest as he yelled. When he turned around, Troy was smiling lazily at him. His eyes were low and he looked drunk as hell. His hair was cut low and he smelled heavenly. The black thermal and black and red cotton pajama pants gave him a very relaxed appearance.

"Boy, you scared the shit out of me. How you got in here?"

"That's what you get since you were supposed to be up waiting for me, and I still have my key. You want it back?"

"You took too long." Alex shook his head. "Just keep it." Alex knew one thing; Troy wasn't the intrusive type. He wouldn't use the key unless instructed to do so.

He smiled. "Un huh. Your ass drunk, ain't you?"

Alex pulled the covers over his face only for Troy to pull them right back down. "Don't be shame now. What you doing up in here drinking?"

"Summer and Rain came over earlier."

"I should have known." The dimples in his cheeks sunk deeper than they'd been.

Alex scooted back until his back was against the headboard. "You know you really look like Jussie Smollett now with your hair cut like that, right?"

Troy ran his hand over his low fade and looked away. "I know. Everybody keeps saying that. He's a hot ass dude, though, so it's cool."

Alex licked his bottom lip and just enjoyed the fact that Troy was sitting near him. He hadn't known he'd missed him that much. In the back of his mind, he knew he loved Troy. He just always felt like he might love Damien more, but in that moment, he was no longer sure. It was like he was seeing him for the first time or something.

"I'm a lil faded, too. You mind if I stay the night?"

Alex pushed the top of his comforter back as an open invitation for Troy to climb in. He scooted over as Troy kicked his shoes off. He walked to the door and flipped the fan on then pulled his shirt over his head. Alex lusted like crazy over his light skin until his eyes landed on that horrible ass unicorn tattoo. He still hated that shit.

"I just want to get a marker and color over that ugly ass tattoo."

Troy laughed and touched the spot on his shoulder where it was. "I'll get it covered up just for you. How about that?"

Alex turned his nose up. "Please do because that shit is just beyond gay."

"You're crazy. You know that, right?"

Alex slid down in the bed. "So I've been told."

Troy hit the lights before joining him in bed. He scooted as close as he could get to Alex and wrapped his arm around him. He laid his head on the pillow before sitting up again.

"You not gon put on that ugly bonnet you be wearing?"

"I wasn't going to, but since you reminded me, can you hand it to me? It's in my top—"

"I know where it's at." Troy got back out the bed and handed Alex the bonnet before getting back in.

Alex tucked all of his long wavy weave into his bonnet and lay back down. As soon as he stopped moving, Troy was right back on him. They snuggled close together and fell asleep. They tossed and turned throughout the night, eventually waking up to a few sessions of lovemaking before the sun came the next morning.

It was nearing eleven o'clock before either of them were fully awake. With a headache the size of his entire apartment, Alex sat up in bed. He was about to go into his kitchen to grab some Tylenol until he saw Troy standing at the bottom of his bed putting his shoes back on.

"You're about to leave?"

He looked up at Alex. "Yeah."

"For real?"

"Yeah. What am I supposed to do?"

Alex shrugged. "I don't know, I just figured you might stay a while."

Troy stood up and grabbed his keys from the dresser. "No. I have to go."

"So, what was last night?"

Troy looked away momentarily before looking back at Alex. "It was what it was. We were drunk, missed each other, and had a weak moment. Nothing more."

"Damn, it's like that?"

"How is it supposed to be? You still haven't made up your mind about me yet, Alex. I had to call you. You didn't call me, nor have you called since the day I left. You don't care about me and I know that. I just got too deep in my feelings last night and slipped. I wanted you to love me like I loved you, but I'm sober again and now I feel like a fool. You still haven't chosen me, so I'm out." Troy didn't bother waiting for an explanation from Alex before leaving.

He walked out of Alex's room and out of his apartment without another thought. Once again, Alex was left to wallow in his depression and uncertainty. As always, he had mixed feelings regarding he and Troy's relationship. But for the first time in months, it had nothing to do with Damien. This time, he was taking full responsibility for it. This was on him. He was the unstable factor in both equations.

Both of them knew what they wanted from him. It was him who didn't know. Alex sat in the same spot for a little while longer before getting out of bed and going into his kitchen. He took two Tylenol and grabbed a bottle of water. He was back in bed and beneath the covers when he got a text.

Damien: I'm coming through today

Alex: Don't bother

Damien: I wasn't asking

Alex: Yes the fuck you were and I said no.

Damien: Fuck it then. You stay on some bullshit

Alex: Whatever

Alex heard his phone beep again, but he didn't even bother to look at it. He didn't care about anything Damien had to say. He was still pissed at him about that shit he pulled on his baby mama's birthday. He had been trying to make it up for weeks, but Alex wasn't trying to hear it. That was so dead. Damien's whole down low life was getting on his nerves.

Instead of worrying himself with Damien and his foolishness, Alex turned his phone on airplane mode and went back to sleep. His head was already hurting, and it looked like Damien wanted nothing more than to make it hurt worse. He'd slept half of the day away by the time his eyes opened again.

He closed his eyes as the sun shone through his curtains and lay still for a minute, trying to wake all the way up. When he felt together, he grabbed his phone and took it off of airplane mode. Before calling anyone else, he dialed Rain. He already knew she had called and was probably having a fit by now.

"Why haven't you been answering? You ain't that drunk. It's almost four o'clock in the afternoon."

"Calm down, mama. I had a late night. I woke up, took some medicine, and fell back to sleep. I had encountered some stupidity before I closed my eyes, so I turned it on airplane mode so I could get some rest. Is that okay with you?"

"You should have text me or something so I would have known."

"Bitchhhhhh," Alex dragged himself from the bed.

He could hear Rain's laughter coming from the other end of the phone. "I'm just trying to make sure your butt is okay. You play so many games, I have to make sure don't nobody come over there and do nothing to your ass."

"Oh, they'll come over here and do something to me alright. As a matter of fact, Troy came over last night and did a whole lot of things to my ass."

Rain screamed. "TMI, BITCH!"

Alex laughed as he urinated. "I probably would still be screaming had the nigga not hopped up and dipped on my ass early."

"Dang, for real? Whose idea was it for him to come over?"

"His. He called me and came over. I woke up this morning about to cook for the nigga with his fine ass, and he went off on me and left. Told me I still want to play, and I'm not ready for him and stuff. Honey, I just looked at him. I couldn't even say nothing. My head was hurting too." Alex sucked his teeth as he washed his hands and left his bathroom.

"Troy means you're going to act right or else."

"I know. That nigga won't even give me a chance to mess up again."

"Got that lil butt and dipped." Rain laughed again.

"Didn't he, though. Then stupid text me talking about he was coming over. Tuh! Nigga in what world? Not mine."

"Good. I'm proud of you. Don't fall for all those straight nigga lies. He's gay, so he need to tell you something you'll believe."

"Die bitch, just die." Alex laughed before he and Rain continued their normal banter for another hour or two, even calling Summer on three way before he hung up.

It was just before six o'clock when he finally left his house. He hadn't been to see his grandma in a few days, so he decided to stop there first. The nursing home she lived in was clean and packed as usual. Since he was going to see his grandmother, he tried to tone down his appearance a little. Not for her, but for all of the other nosey ass old people she lived with.

She knew him and loved him the same, but he still did his best to keep it calm. He'd worn a straight pair of blue jeans and a plain white fitted t-shirt. His hair was pulled back into a ponytail and he wore large silver hoop earrings. He hadn't put on any makeup, so he slid his large black shades over his face and walked to her room.

When he pushed the door open, there was an older gentleman sitting next to her. He looked to be around his grandmother's age and was smiling as large as his wrinkly old skin would allow. His brown skin and white hair resembled Alex's grandmother. When they'd heard the door open, they both looked at him. His granny smiled while the old man just nodded his head.

"There goes my baby." She held both of her hands out toward him.

Alex walked right to her and kissed her forehead, before leaning down to hug her. "Hey, sexy. What you doing with this man up in here?"

His grandma smiled bashfully, before tapping his shoulder. "Oh, you stop it. This here is Randy. Randy, this is my beautiful baby, Alex. Alex, take your glasses off and say hello, baby."

Alex didn't take orders from anyone but his granny. He'd do whatever she told him to do with no hesitation. He removed his glasses and stuck them into his purse before setting it on the floor. He stretched his hand out toward Randy, but all he did was look at it.

"Oh, my. You're a boy?" he asked once he could see Alex's face clearly. "Emma Jean, you didn't tell me the Alex you're always talking about was a boy."

"So?" His granny looked at her friend like she had an attitude.

Randy didn't even bother to address her. He looked at Alex instead. "You are a boy, and you need to act like one. Wearing all this girl stuff is not going to make you a woman. You're just a pervert."

"Randy, get your ass out of my room." Emma Jean scolded.

"It's okay, Granny, he can stay. I'm not bothered."

"No he can't either. Get out of here, you old fool."

"Gladly." Randy hobbled to his feet and scooted out of the room with his cane.

Alex thought about sticking his foot out and tripping him up but figured he may never heal so he changed his mind. Once the room to her door closed, she grabbed Alex's hand.

"I'm sorry, baby."

"It's okay for real, Granny. I'm used to it."

"You shouldn't have to be. That's one of the main reasons I tell you to let this go. People don't see you for who you are. All they care about is the outside. They don't know my sweet boy in here." His granny tapped his chest.

Alex sat on the carpeted floor near her feet and lay his head back against her knees. She rubbed his head and scratched his scalp like she'd been doing since he was a child.

"How are you feeling today?"

"Good as these old bones will let me feel. I haven't seen you in a while. What's going on?"

"I've just been busy with work and stuff." He was almost about to tell her about the fire at Rain's house, but he caught himself. He didn't want to worry her. She was old, and the smallest thing would send her over the edge.

She patted his shoulder. "I understand, baby. It's okay. It ain't nothing going on in here anyway."

"I can't tell. It looks like a lot going on with you and Randy's old ass."

His granny laughed as she went back to rubbing his head. He didn't know why, but she always got a kick out of him cussing. He tried his best to never take it too far because he respected her, but he still did just enough to make her laugh.

"He's just my friend."

"Um huh. That's what they all say."

"How are your friends? I can't remember their names. The good one and the other one."

Alex smiled because he knew she was referring to Damien and Troy. "They're okay. One doesn't want me because he says I don't want him, then there's the other one who doesn't have a clue what he wants."

"Well, in my opinion, all of y'all are confused. All of y'all think y'all want each other, and that just ain't right. Y'all need some women, baby. Not each other. That's a sin."

"Granny…"

"I know you don't want to hear it, but I'mma say it anyway because I love you."

"I know, I've been thinking about going to church lately. I'm just scared because you know how church people can be."

"You can't let that stop you. God is the only one you need to worry about pleasing."

"I just don't want people looking at me and stuff."

His granny pushed his shoulder playfully. "Yes, you do. You've always wanted people to look at you. I think that's half the reason you call yourself liking men."

Alex shook his head at his granny. She would say anything. He stayed with her for a little while longer before he announced he was leaving. She was sad to see him go, but he promised to come back soon. With his purse on his shoulder and his shades over his face, he left her room. In the lobby, he saw Randy standing near the nurse's station.

When he passed by, he heard him saying something that sounded like Alex should be ashamed of himself or something like that. Alex wasn't going to say anything, but he'd let him slide the first time. This time, he turned around and walked over to him.

"What did your old ass say to me?"

"I said you need to be ashamed of yourself for acting like a woman."

"Let me tell you something, you old wrinkled balls fucker. I am grown and can do what the fuck I want. That includes dating boys. So take my advice, the next time you see me, keep it moving before I rub my dick across your old ass lips." Alex smiled at the look on Randy's face. "Was that manly enough for you?" He winked at Randy before walking away.

He could hear the nurses at the station laughing as he headed for the door. He even snickered to himself some. He probably didn't have to be so disrespectful, but some old people just brought it out of you. They thought because they were old that they could say what they wanted, and they probably could. Just not to Alex.

When he got into his car, he called Summer. "Hey, what you doing?"

"Getting ready to go to Jacorey's house."

"You take advantage of your weekends off, don't you?"

"Boy, yeah. Those kids be having me running all week long. I be glad when the end of the week gets here."

Alex turned his car out of the parking lot. "What you and Jacorey about to do?"

"Nothing for real, why?"

"I was just about to see did you want to go to the mall with me. I need to get some white jeans for this hair magazine photo shoot I have coming up."

"Yeah, I'll go. I can go see Jacorey later."

"Cool. I'm about to come get you."

Alex and Summer hung up. He drove the whole way to Summer's spot singing along with his music. A few minutes after he text her to let her know he was outside, she was out the door. The burgundy dress she was wearing made her look ten times better than she already did. Summer was a bad ass female, and he was gay, so he could see why she had all the straight niggas choosing.

She bounced happily to his car and got in. "Heyyyy, best friend.

"Hey, boo. Put your seatbelt on."

Summer grabbed her seatbelt and locked it as Alex pulled out of her parking lot. They talked about a little bit of everything as they drove to the mall. They weren't surprised that it was packed, being that it was Saturday. Peachtree Mall stayed packed on the weekends. Once Alex found a park, they got out and headed inside.

They went from store to store looking for Alex the perfect all white outfit for his pictures. They were in H&M when they finally found something that he could work with. Alex stepped out of the dressing room for Summer to see the pants.

"Yes. I like those." She held her thumb up.

"What about my butt. It ain't sticking too far out, is it?" Alex looked at himself in the body length mirror behind him.

"No, honey. Those pants are fierce," some boy who had just come out of the dressing room next to his said.

Alex and Summer both looked at him. He was a skinny little black boy with tight clothes on. They fit a little too snug for Alex's liking, but he made up for it with his makeup. His face was made up beautifully and he had a long blonde weave. Alex probably wouldn't have picked the blonde for him, but it was done so he couldn't say much.

"You think so?" Alex asked.

"I do. And so what if your butt sticks out? That's a good thing, queen." He snapped and put his hand on his hip.

Summer snapped playfully and put her hand on her hip as well. "Well, queen, the crowd has spoken. Now go take them damn pants off so we can go. It's too many lil children up in this mall. I think I saw one of my students."

Alex and the boy both laughed at Summer. Alex turned toward the boy. "Thank you."

"No problem, my love." He air kissed Alex before leaving the dressing room.

When Alex was completely dressed and had the pants thrown across his arm, he and Summer walked out of the room.

"Baby was high maintenance, honey," Summer said, referring to the boy from the dressing room.

"Baby needed to get rid of that blonde hair and them tight ass clothes."

Summer giggled as she nodded her head. "You ain't lying."

"Then had the nerve to think I was going to take his advice on some clothes." Alex and Summer huddled together laughing as they walked down the aisle.

"We ain't even right talking about that boy like that. He was nice."

"Yeah, he was. He just needed some nicer weave and nicer hair." Alex said, making her laugh again.

She was still laughing as he turned around to get a different pair of the white pants. He never bought the clothes he tried on. He always had to get a new pair in his size. He was still pushing through the racks when he felt Summer discreetly tapping his back.

"Don't look now, but I think Troy is in here with Mr. Go-Go Diva."

Alex disregarded everything Summer had said about not looking and spun completely around. As soon as he did, he came face to face with Troy. He was standing near the rack of clothes the boy was sifting through. When he saw Alex, his face gave him away. He looked caught as he began fidgeting with his hands.

"Can you believe this nigga?"

"I mean, Alex, it has been a while since y'all broke up."

Alex looked at Summer. "It may have been, but it ain't been but a few hours since the last time he got this ass."

Summer's eyes bucked. "He came over there last night?"

Alex nodded. "That's probably why he over there looking crazy. Scared I'mma tell on his ass." Alex sucked his teeth. "He could have done better than that nigga. He around here making me feel bad about not choosing him and shit, and he's up in here sporting America's Next Top Sissy. I can't believe this shit." Alex turned back around and began sifting through the clothes again.

He tried his best not to let Troy's actions get the best of him, but he couldn't help himself. He sniffed continuously trying to keep his tears at bay, but it was getting harder and harder by the second. When Summer finally noticed what he was doing, she walked closer to him and grabbed his chin. She turned his whole face toward her and looked into his eyes.

"Stop this shit. Stop it now. You will not stand in this mall and cry about no nigga. Especially one you don't even want. Get yourself together."

Alex nodded and tried to pull his face away, but Summer held on to it. "You're going to be fine, boo. You hear me? You are fine."

Alex nodded again, still unable to speak, and turned back around. His constant fidgeting must have annoyed Summer because she looked through the rack and grabbed his size. She then grabbed his hand and pulled him toward the register. They stood in line waiting to be rung up. He was looking around trying to avoid Summer, but she was staring at him hard as hell trying to make sure he didn't cry.

Alex wanted to say something smart, but at the moment, he really couldn't. He didn't have anything left to say. He was so used to Troy always being there no matter what. Now to see him out with somebody else made him question not only himself and Troy but everything they'd been through as well. All the things Troy had ever told him. Including the fact that he loved him because that had to be a lie. There was no way that he would be out in public flossing the next nigga if he did.

"So, you're getting the pants, boo?" Alex and Summer looked at each other before turning around to face the boy.

Summer narrowed her eyes at Alex, letting him know not to start no shit before he turned completely around.

"Yeah," Alex said dryly.

"Good. They were really cute."

"I keep trying to tell him that it doesn't matter what he wears, he has so much style he can pull off whatever it is he chooses to wear." Summer tried to intervene to lighten the mood.

"Say that, honey. I love a supportive sister."

"Me too," Alex said, looking past him to Troy.

"Troy, hey boo." Summer stepped around the boy and hugged Troy.

He hugged her back and kissed her cheek. "How you doing, Summer? You look gorgeous as always, my love."

"Thank you, boo. I'm good. Still dealing with all my bad kids."

Troy nodded his head at her. She was sure in appreciation for her efforts in mellowing out the mood. "You got it. You're a hard ass. I know you can handle it."

"You know I can." She smiled. "It was nice seeing you, boo. Don't be a stranger now. You know we're better than that."

"I'll do my best."

Summer stepped back around the boy and stood back next to Alex. She could see the questioning eyes Troy's little friend was giving them both, but she ignored them. If he knew like she did, he would take that up with Troy and not her. She would most definitely fuck him up for being with her best friend's man.

"You make me sick," Alex told her once they got to the register.

"So. He was getting on my nerves talking to you."

"Girl, mine too. I didn't know how much more I was going to be able to take. I'm sure you know that already, though."

Summer talked to him the rest of the time they were in the store. They had walked out and were headed down the mall when they heard someone calling Summer's name. When they turned around, it was the boy. He sped walked to them and touched Alex' arm.

"What's your name?"

"Why?" Alex got into defense mode.

"I just want to know."

"It's Alex, why?" Summer interrupted.

He pointed his finger and nodded his head. "I knew it was you. He really loved you, ya know?" The boy smiled and began backing up. "Thank you for messing up, though."

Summers' grip on his arm was the only thing that stopped Alex from making a fool of himself in the mall.

"Don't. Just don't. It's not that serious. He's just being messy."

Alex's breathing had picked up as water began to cloud his vision. "Let's just go."

Summer agreed that it was time to go, so she looped her arm through his and they exited the mall. After dropping Summer back off, Alex went back home and tried his best to evaluate his life and the choices that needed to be made.

Chapter 10: Why Me?

Fallon pulled Jazz from the back seat of her car and bumped the door closed with her hip. She hit the locks and headed for the stairs to her sister-in-law's house. Because her husband was due back in town the next morning and she didn't really feel like driving all the way home, she figured her easiest alibi would be to just crash at his family's house.

Though she was sure she was finally ready to call it quits, she wanted to do it on her own terms. Arguing and fussing about her not being in Albany while he was gone would surely make that hard. With Jazz' body thrown over her shoulder, Fallon walked to the door. Like she told her she would be, Iesha was in the doorway waiting for her.

She pulled the door completely open and allowed them to walk in. "Hey, boo. You already know the way." She ushered Fallon to the guest bedroom.

"Thanks so much, girl."

"No problem. Everything is all set for y'all. See you in the morning." Iesha closed the door to the small bedroom and left.

She was the sweetest thing while her brother could be mean as a rattlesnake. Fallon set her purse and her and Jazz' overnight bag down on the chair, before kicking her shoes off. She then pulled the covers back and laid him on the bed. Dakota had already given him a bath and put his pajamas on, so he was good for the night.

Once he was settled, she changed her clothes, wrapped her hair, and got into bed with him. She was knocked out and calling hogs before she knew it. The next morning, she woke up to a baby crying. She knew it had to be Nyla. Iesha had just given birth to her a few months ago, and all she complained about was how much Nyla cried.

Fallon smiled to herself as she rose from the bed. Even though it was only a little after eight o'clock, she still knew it was time for her to get on the road. She changed her clothes and gathered all of their things. Jazz could keep on his pajamas. She unwrapped her hair, threw her scarf back in her bag, and grabbed her baby.

Jazz woke up as soon as she touched him. He wrapped both of his arms around her legs and laid his head against her thighs.

"Sit right here, man, and let Mommy make up the bed." She sat Jazz on the futon in the corner and made the bed.

Once the room was back how it had been when she came in, Fallon threw her things over her shoulder and picked Jazz up. She opened the door, stepping on various toys, and made her way down the hallway. When she got into the kitchen, she noticed Iesha sitting at the table with the baby. She was feeding her a jar of baby food.

"I'm out, boo."

Iesha turned around. "Dang, already?"

"Girl, yeah. You know your brother gets back today and he's going to want Jazz and me there."

"I understand, boo. Just call me when you get there."

"I will." Fallon walked out of the kitchen, then left the house.

She made sure to buckle Jazz in his car seat before throwing their bags in and hopping in the driver' seat. Once her music was on, she was ready to ride. The hour and a half drive to Albany from Columbus wasn't bad, but it wasn't one she cared for. All she could think about was how soon it would all be over.

Now that she had cleared everything up with Dakota and made things right, she had a new outlook on life. Initially, she'd just wanted to make things right so that if her health ever took a turn for the worst that he would take Jazz for her. Her husband was an okay father and could probably take care of Jazz, but only once he was ready.

He wasn't ready yet. He still had a lot of single man priorities he hadn't let go of yet, and she didn't want her baby to be neglected. His father was always going somewhere and doing something, Jazz would probably live with Iesha if something were to happen to her. She trusted Iesha and loved her a lot, but she had her own kids and man to deal with.

Fallon didn't want Jazz anywhere where he would be mistreated or not given enough attention. She hadn't known for sure, but she'd always felt that Dakota would be the perfect person for him. He would still be able to tell Jazz about her and their parents while giving him a good home. After staying with them for the weekend, she was even more sure of her decision now.

The love Dakota and Rain showed Jazz was crazy. Especially since they hadn't even known him long. She'd had to promise everything except her life for Dakota to even let him leave with her this time. Fallon smiled as she thought about how much more Jazz looked like Dakota than his own father. Now that was crazy. What was even crazier was the fact that he had been looking like him since birth.

The time spent with her brother and his circle had been just what she'd needed to get her back on track. They'd given her so much life in just one short weekend. She could only imagine what it would be like once she moved to Columbus permanently. She and Jazz would finally have a family. Something she was sure they'd both been longing for.

"Are we there yet, Mommy? I see the lights," Jazz said, from the backseat.

Fallon laughed to herself as she thought about the lights he was referring to. They were the large ones from the gas station down the street from their house. She thought it was cute how he used it to recognize that they were almost home.

"Yep. Almost there."

Fallon turned her car onto their street and continued driving. She passed four more houses before turning into her driveway. Her husband's truck was already parked along the street, so she knew he was home. She rolled her eyes in anticipation for what was to come. All he did was complain. Like he had any room to do so. After she turned her car off she got out, grabbed their bags and then opened the door for Jazz. He unlocked his seat belt and hopped out.

He grabbed her hand as they walked down the driveway to the front door. She used her key to let them in before closing the door behind herself. Jazz walked down the hall, to his room she assumed. With all of their bags still on her shoulder, she headed to her room as well. She could smell the smoke before she even opened the door.

When she opened it, her husband, Drake was lying across the bed in his boxers watching TV and smoking a cigarette.

"What have I told you about smoking in the house?"

He took another puff from his cigarette and blew out the smoke. "How you come in the house tripping?"

"Because I came in and you're doing the very thing I've asked you not to do a million times."

"Well, I've asked you to have your ass at home when I'm away, but you don't do what I tell you, so shid..." He blew out some more smoke. "I guess we're both two hard-headed muthafuckas."

"Whatever." Fallon waved him off and walked into her bathroom.

She hadn't taken a bath the night before at Dakota's house because she was on her cycle, and with her disease, she always tried to be extra careful. She turned the shower on and began taking off of her clothes. She was naked from the waist up when the door opened. Drake came in with a frown on his face, which gained him one right back in return.

Fallon turned her nose up. "What?"

"Why the first thing you do when you walk in the door is take a shower?"

"Boy, if you don't get your behind out of here with that mess."

Drake grabbed her arm. "I'm not playing with you, Fallon."

"And I'm not playing with you either. Get your hand off of me. You've got some nerve coming in here talking to me, with all the shit you do. Hell, if I did want another nigga, you made sure to ruin that for me."

Drake cowered once those words left her mouth. As he always did because he knew not only was it the truth, but he knew he was wrong for doing it. He looked her up and down as she bucked her eyes at him, waiting for him to get out. Once the door closed fully, she looked at herself in the mirror. She pushed her dress down the rest of her body so that she was naked.

Anytime she would look at herself and think about how perfect she was she would start feeling bad. You would never know that she was terminally ill just by looking at her. Her shape was banging, her face was pretty, and she looked healthy. Nothing about her said AIDS, but the paper the doctor had given her.

It was so crazy to her, but she'd found a way to deal with it so she wouldn't let it get her down today. Fallon reached under her sink to grab her shower cap and slid it on her head. She stepped into the shower and slid down to the floor, allowing the water to massage her tired body. She didn't know how long she stayed in the shower, but once the water started to get cold, she got out.

Being that she hadn't brought anything in the bathroom with her, she had to leave the bathroom in her towel. Drake was back in his spot on the bed with his phone in his hand. She rolled her eyes and continued to her closet. She didn't even care who he was talking to. Whatever hoe it was, she was nasty, or on her way to being sick.

Fallon wished she could tattoo his forehead with the word AIDS so that every woman he came in contact with could go the other way. It wasn't fair to them, just like it hadn't been fair to her.

"I don't know why you don't just leave them girls alone. You ain't gon do nothing but end their lives early." Fallon walked past the bed with her panties and tights.

She was closing the bathroom door when she heard him say fuck her. She smiled and put her clothes on then grabbed one of her bras that was hanging on the bathroom door and put it on before exiting again.

Back in her room, she grabbed her laptop and sat on the bed. "Jazz," she yelled.

She watched her screen until the picture of her and Jazz popped up on her desktop. She scrolled to the internet and opened it up.

"Yes, ma'am?" Jazz came around the corner.

"What you doing?"

"Watching Spy Kids on Netflix."

"Oh, okay, well go ahead. I just wanted to see what you were doing." Fallon smiled at him and he took off running from the room.

"What you looking up apartments for?" Drake asked her.

"None of your business. I'm looking for a divorce attorney next, though. Now that, you can worry about."

Drake sat up in bed and looked at her. "The hell you been this weekend that got you acting all brand new and shit?"

"Again, I'll tell you, none of your business," Fallon said, in her most sarcastic tone.

Drake snatched her computer as she got the number to the apartments Rain had taken her to price.

"What you think you're doing?"

"Leaving your ass."

"No, the fuck you ain't."

"Yes, my dear, I am. Now give me my computer back please."

Fallon knew her sarcasm would get next to him and she was glad. Something needed to get to his black ass. Clearly her complaining about being lonely and sad didn't, so maybe this would.

"Fallon, you're not taking my son anywhere."

"Why I'm not? You never see him anyway. You moved us here, and you've been gone off doing your own thing ever since."

"I be working." He got indignant.

"Yeah, baby, I'm sure you do."

"Fallon, stop playing so much."

"I'm not playing, baby. I'm so serious right now. Probably the most serious I've been in all of my life. I'm tired of your cheating ass."

Fallon held her hand up for him when she noticed her cell phone ringing on the dresser. She picked it up and answered. It was Iesha.

"Hey boo, what's up?"

Fallon could hear a lot of noise in the background before Iesha's voice became clearer. "You're the one that keeps cheating. If you would just leave all those other bitches alone, then I wouldn't be tripping. You stupid fucker!" she yelled.

Fallon pulled the phone away from her ear until Iesha stopped yelling. "Iesha!"

"Yeah. My bad, girl. I'm just so tired of this nigga. He stays out with that bitch all night then comes home like I don't know. That bastard gets on my nerves. I don't know what it is about this same girl that he can't seem to get enough of."

"Girl, you're preaching to the choir. Your brother on the same shit."

"What's wrong with these niggas, sis?" Iesha asked.

"I wish I knew," Fallon told her.

In no rush to get back to the conversation she'd been having with Drake, Fallon sat on the phone with Iesha for another thirty minutes, comparing the dirt their men did. Which wasn't out of the norm. They had their own private vent sessions at least once a month. By the time she got off the phone, Drake was sitting on the bed looking at her like a timid child would look at their mother.

He must have finally realized that she was serious because he stopped trying to act hard. "Baby, come on. Don't do this. I told you I stopped all that."

Fallon looked at him. "Oh, you did, huh?"

"Yeah boo, I did."

Fallon held her hand out toward him. "Well let me see your phone."

Drake looked down at it, then back up at her. "You're supposed to trust me. How we gon be together if you don't trust me?"

"See, you're a liar. You can't let me see it because you're lying, but it's cool. I don't give a damn. My baby and I are leaving your ass. You can stay right here in this country ass town and continue on doing whatever it is that you've been doing."

"I don't want to do that. I want to be with you." He set her computer back down in front of her and she grabbed it quickly.

"Thank you." Fallon went back to her apartment search.

She stayed on there long enough to get the necessary numbers before switching the website to the local job listings. She was not about to keep playing with Drake. He could take his sick, cheating ass somewhere and kick rocks. She was tired, and she was done with his games.

*****

Love lay on the black weight bench pushing the bar up and down over his head. He took deep breaths and pushed over and over until he reached fifty. Richardson was behind him waiting to spot him if need be, but he hadn't needed it. Working out was nothing new to him. He had been doing it for years.

"Damn, boy. What you ate this morning? Some Wheaties?" Richardson stuck his hand out for dap as Love stood from the bench.

Love slapped his hand with Richardson's before grabbing his towel to wipe the sweat from his face.

"Nah, nigga, I'm just a beast like that."

"Hell, nah. Rain probably at your house fixing you Raisin Brand and protein bars for breakfast and shit. When you was living by yourself, you weren't knocking down no iron like that." Richardson referred to the weights Love had just been lifting.

Love laughed and pulled his locs out of the ponytail they were in. "This dude."

He walked behind the bench and took the place Richardson had just occupied. He looked straight ahead as Richardson lifted the weights.

"Yo, man, you still ain't figured out who was doing that shit to your girl?"

Love shook his head. "Nah, I been trying my hardest. I got cameras and everything set up at the crib, but ain't shit happened since she been with me."

"She don't know who it was?"

"She said it was some woman, but she ain't never seen the chick before. That shit just doesn't make any sense to me, though. I don't fuck with nobody but her. The other bitches that I had a few run-ins with she knows what they look like. So I don't know."

Richardson lifted the bar above his head again. "You sure you ain't got no crazy ex's or no shit like that?"

Love shook his head slowly as he tried to think of all of the women in his past. "I don't. I mean, there's my ex, Tocara, but she ain't with no shit like that. She's actually about to marry her nigga, I think. She shouldn't be worried about my ass or the woman I'm with."

"Well, you need to get a hold on that shit before it gets out of control again. If they were crazy enough to do some shit like that the last time, it ain't no telling what depths they may go to this time."

Love nodded his head in agreement because he had thought of the same thing. He and Rain had already taken all of the necessary precautions. Going to the police, filing reports, and installing alarm systems in his house and on her car. With neither of them really knowing the girl or where she'd come from, their hands were kind of tired.

There wasn't much that they could do. "I'mma try to check on some more shit when I get home. Maybe show her some pictures of some of my old hoes or something, to see if she can recognize somebody."

Richardson placed the bar back on the holder and sat up. "Yeah, do that. Nothing fails but a try."

Love tossed him a clean towel and headed into the building to grab his phone. When he picked it up, he saw that he had two missed calls from Rain. He called her right back.

"What's up, baby doll?"

"Nothing. I'm just bored. What you doing."

"Bored. Halfway hoping a fire will break out somewhere."

Rain giggled. "We should be bored together. What you think?"

"I think so, too. You on your way?"

"Yep."

"Cool. Well, hit me when you get here."

Love hung up his phone and dropped it down in his pocket. He walked to the front of the building and sat down, waiting for Rain to call back. The sun was shining and it was a beautiful day out. He stretched his legs out in front of him and took a deep breath. The days were getting shorter and it seemed as if he and Rain were getting nowhere with her attacker.

It frustrated him, but he didn't let it show. His uneasiness would only worry her, and he didn't want that. Not while she was pregnant anyway. He smiled as he thought about them having a baby. She was still too early to tell what they were having, but he couldn't wait. He was secretly hoping for a little girl, especially since he had Jazz now.

In a weird way, he felt like Jazz was his boy. He still wanted a son of his own one day, but as of right now, all he wanted was a little girl to steal his heart like her mother had. Hopefully, Fallon would be a woman of her word and continue to bring him around. She seemed to be sincere about her apology and wanting to rebuild their relationship so he would remain optimistic for now. If she looked the least bit shady, he was going to have to cut her off the same way she'd done him. He would hate to do it, but he was too old for the past to repeat itself.

Love's vibrating phone brought him out of his thoughts. It was Rain. "I'm already outside waiting for you."

"Dakota!" She sounded scared.

"Rain? What's wrong?"

"I just got into a car accident, but I don't think it was an accident. The car kept bumping my car from the back so I tried to turn off and lose it. They followed me and hit me again. I ran into a tree and my back and head hurt so bad." She lost her composure toward the end and started crying.

"Fuck man! Where you at?"

"Around the street from you. Near the Popeye's chicken."

"Okay, we're on the way. Stay on the phone." Love ran to the back and alerted his team of what happened. They all looked like they were just as shocked and afraid as he was.

Instead of waiting for them, he took off running to where she was. His station was literally in walking distance from the Popeye's chicken that she'd just mentioned. He held the phone in his hand the entire time he ran. She was on speakerphone, so he could still hear her crying. She wasn't loud, just soft whimpers and moans.

He could hear her voice faintly saying stuff about their baby being okay. The heat beat down on him and his dreads flew back as he ran. He was breathing hard and could feel every muscle in his body at work. He sprinted down the back street the fire department was on until he was on the main street.

Though he couldn't see Rain's car, he could see a few other cars pulled over alongside the road, as well as smoke in the air. The sirens from his team's firetruck were in the near distance. He could tell they were right behind him, but none of them would get there before him. Love looked both ways before darting across the street. He didn't need to injure himself before making sure Rain was okay.

"Excuse me! Let me through." Love yelled as he pushed his way through the crowd.

The phone in his hand was shoved into his pocket the moment he saw her. Her door was open and there was a tall white man kneeling next to the car. He was holding her hand and saying something to her. Love couldn't hear him, but he was just happy she wasn't alone.

"Rain," Love kneeled next to the man. "How you feeling? Can you feel your legs?"

"Yes," she said, weakly. "You got here fast... my head hurts." She closed her eyes momentarily.

"Open your eyes, Rain. You have to stay awake and talk to me." Love stood to his feet and leaned as far into her car as he could. Which wasn't much, being that the airbag was out. He tried to see as much as he could to figure out how they would have to get her out without causing further damage.

"There's the firetruck." Someone yelled from behind him.

"He's a firefighter as well, ladies and gentlemen. Let's say we give these gentlemen some room." The man who had been kneeling next to Rain stood up and began motioning the crowd backward with his hands.

Love's attire must have given him away. Either that or Rain had told him before he'd gotten there. Whatever it was didn't matter as much right then. Love squatted back down and held Rain's hand as his team members ran up beside him. Had they been any other men he probably would have wanted to handle this all on his own, but he trusted this group of men with his own life.

Not to mention they had been there for the first attempt on Rain's life, so they all knew how hard this must have been for him. Rain's head was leaning to the side with shattered glass fragments in her hair and skin. There was blood coming from a cut on her forehead, and judging from the angle of her arm, it was probably broken.

"Can she feel her legs?" Richardson kneeled next to Rain with a large blue bag in his hand.

Love told him yes at the same time that Rain nodded her head. Her long brown legs were still tucked snugly between the low dashboard and the large air bag in front of her. Her left arm was dangling down and her mouth was slightly open. His baby doll was in bad shape all over again, and he still hadn't done anything to solve it.

Love took a deep breath and turned toward the other members of his crew that were coming forward with various tools to help release Rain from the car. The whole ordeal felt like forever, but in reality, it had only been minutes. Love, along with the help of Richardson and Rodriguez, two of his most trusted friends, managed to pull Rain from the car without any further injuries.

By that time, the paramedics had arrived. As bad as Love just wanted to hold her in his arms, he couldn't do that at the moment.

However, he was able to cradle her for just a few seconds as he walked her to the waiting stretcher. During this brief moment of contact, he noticed the blood running down Rain's legs.

He didn't want to believe that was a sign of his baby's life drifting from her, but he had been in this exact situation a few times before due to his job. He sighed and bit his bottom lip to keep the tears from falling as he placed her on the stretcher. The moment she was on it securely, the paramedics pushed her off to the back of the ambulance with Love in tow.

She was in and out of consciousness as they rode to the hospital. Unlike the first time they'd been in the back of an ambulance together, Love was weak. Versus assisting in her care, he sat back exhausted and depressed. He watched them do what they could for her until the truck came to a stop.

When the doors opened, he hopped out and followed behind them hopelessly. They were in the emergency room for a while before Summer and Alex arrived. He'd called Summer once they took Rain to the back and asked him to remain outside. Being that this felt like déjà vu, they were all pretty much in the same state, a bit withdrawn, but very concerned. Anger and uncertainty hung in the air as they waited to be informed of Rain's condition. She had been lucky enough to make it last time, hopefully, it would be the same this time around.

Chapter 11: Sneaky Strangers

Rain sat in the rocking chair on Love's small porch and rocked back and forth. The sun was shining and the day was one of the most beautiful days she'd seen in a long time. As nice as the day was, it was the complete opposite of Rain's mood. She had been in a slump since the day she'd lost her baby and still hadn't come out of it.

Though she hadn't been that far along in her pregnancy, she'd still grown attached to her child. It had been two weeks and her heart ached like it had been two minutes. Everyone in her circle had been going out of their way to make her feel better, but nothing was helping. Summer, Alex, Love, and Fallon had been showering her with attention and gifts, but nothing mattered. Fallon had even called her earlier to let her know she was coming into town, but not even that excited her.

All she could think about was who could hate her enough to continue to ruin her life. One minute she was talking to Alex about him falling weak and sleeping with Damien again, and the next she was smashed into a tree. Whoever it was had taken almost everything she had when they burned her apartment down, but now that she'd lost her baby as well, she could hardly think straight. She had practically fried her brain to death trying to think of who it might be, and she continued to come up with nothing.

Rain had no enemies. She'd been nothing but nice to anyone that she came in contact with, but clearly that didn't matter. To make matters worse, the last day she was in the hospital someone had slid a note under her door, but by the time she recognized it was there, they were gone. She saw no one other than the nurses.

Love had the police take a look at the tapes of the floor she was on, but nothing looked out of the ordinary. People had passed it all day long and they couldn't point out just one individual who could have been the attacker. It angered Love, but it depressed Rain further. Would this ever end? She was beginning to think that it wouldn't.

"Baby doll, you have to eat." Love walked out of the house in his work clothes and carrying his bag.

The chicken pasta and lemonade he'd given her earlier was still sitting there, along with her laptop and notebook. Everything was in the exact place he'd left it, leading him to the conclusion that she hadn't touched anything. As she hadn't the other few times he'd tried to feed her or get her to write.

"I'm not hungry right now."

"That's all you ever say."

"Well, maybe you should believe me." Rain looked at him.

His hair was freshly twisted and hanging down his back He had his locs tied back with a band, keeping them out of his face.

"Rain, I know you're sad, baby, but you can't do this. You have to stop. Your depression is getting out of control. If you don't start trying to do better, I'm going to make you come with me to work every day or I'm going to hire someone to sit in and watch you all day. The choice is yours."

Love kissed her face and walked away.

Rain wanted to yell and scream at him that she was hurting. She needed him to understand that she wanted food, she wanted to write, she just couldn't. Every time she tried, she thought about her baby. She knew she needed to get herself together, but she didn't want to right now. She wanted to be sad. Rain needed the world to stop and feel her pain. It wasn't fair that she was the only one that had to hurt. She would give anything to be on the phone making fun of Alex about being Damien's fool again. Had she been paying attention that day, her baby might still be alive.

With her arms folded across her chest, Rain's eyes rolled in Love's direction as he backed out of his driveway. He gave her a stern look before pulling away and driving down the street. Rain only pouted for a few more minutes before snatching her phone from the small table near where she was sitting and called Summer.

It was a little after twelve o'clock so she should have been at lunch by now. Rain patted her foot impatiently against the porch as she waited for Summer to answer.

"Heyy, Rain."

"Hey."

"What you doing, baby?" Summer sang, playfully.

"Nothing."

"You feeling okay today?"

"No."

Summer sighed. "Well, what's wrong?"

"Dakota. He keeps rushing me to get better and acting like nothing ever happened. It's like he doesn't even care."

"He cares, Rain, but you have to understand he's a man. You two are going to deal with this differently. As far as him rushing you, I don't think it's like that. I think he wants you to get a grip on your life, not necessarily forget what happened."

"Do you agree with him?"

Summer yelled at some of her students before giving Rain her attention again. "Yes, I do. I understand it hurts, but you can't die too, Rain. It probably wouldn't be as bad if you were trying to get better. You're not even trying."

Rain could feel herself on the verge of tears, but she held them in. "I don't know how."

"Get your ass out that house for one. Secondly, get your gotdamn hair combed. Bitch, you look terrible."

Rain laughed for the first time since the accident. She laughed so hard she began to cry tears. She hadn't known it, but it was a laugh she had needed.

"Man, fuck you, Summer."

Summer joined her laughter. "I'm just trying to help you out. That boy probably tired of you looking like some kind of crackhead."

"I don't look that bad." Rain ran her hand over her head.

"Yes, bitch, you do."

Rain laughed again. "Well, let me call Alex to see can he do my hair. You make me sick."

"Well hurry up, honey, because I can't take too many more days of you looking like that."

Rain and Summer laughed some more before ending their call. Rain dialed Alex as soon as they hung up.

"Well if it ain't the walking dead." Alex's voice made Rain smile.

"I ain't no damn walking dead, bitch."

"The hell you say."

"You and Summer get on my nerves."

"Bitch, your dirty ass hair and them raggedy ass pajamas should get on your damn nerves because they sure as hell get on mine every time I come over there."

Rain giggled in amusement. "Why you have to be so rude all the time?"

"I'm not rude, I'm real. Now, what pulled you back to reality?"

"Dakota. He said he was going to make me go to work with him every day if I didn't get myself together."

"Whew! Thank goodness he finally took charge. If I was his ass, you would have been outside on your damn neck. I wouldn't be walking around my house every day looking at your ass like that."

"I am not that bad."

Alex sucked his teeth. "Let you tell it."

"Whatever. Can you do my hair today?"

"Yeah. Come on."

Rain rolled her eyes and almost slipped back into depression. "I don't have a car, remember?"

Alex got quiet. "Oh dang. My bad. I'm on the way. Just be ready when I pull up."

After that they hung up, Rain gathered her things and went into the house. She got into the shower and cleaned herself quickly before dressing in a short sundress and sandals. Her hair was oily and a mess, so she just brushed it back into a ball. She wasn't in the mood to do too much, so instead of putting on a lot of jewelry she opted for a simple pair of earrings instead.

She thought about making up the bed and getting her clothes out of the floor before leaving but changed her mind. She wasn't in that good of a mood. Maybe after getting her hair done and maybe even her nails and toes, she would feel better. For now, she grabbed her purse, phone, and keys and headed for the door.

She was in the kitchen setting the alarm when she heard Alex beeping the horn. Once she walked outside, she pulled the door up behind her and headed to Alex's truck. He gave her his best smile when she got in.

"Stop smiling at me like that, Alex, it makes you look straight."

He rolled his eyes and pulled away. "Never."

Rain laughed and sat back in her seat. She looked out of the window not saying anything as he drove.

"You actually don't even look as bad as you did yesterday."

Rain cut her eyes at him as he pulled into the parking lot of the local shopping center. "Where we going?"

"Do you not see your eyebrows and that cracked pink polish on your hand? You need to do something about that."

Rain touched her eyebrows and shook her head. He was right. She did look a mess. "Okay, let's do it."

They were getting out of the car when Alex tapped Rain's shoulder. "Ain't that Fallon?"

Rain followed Alex's finger. "Yeah, that's her. She told me she was coming down today."

Fallon was coming out of the Winn Dixie grocery store when Rain and Alex saw her. Rain briefly wondered where Jazz was since she was alone.

"Heyyy, Fallon girl," Alex waved at her across the parking lot.

Her head spun around when she heard her name. She smiled brightly when she saw them. Without saying another word, she switched quickly over to them. She grabbed Rain in a tight hug as soon as she was close enough. She probably still would have been hugging her if Alex hadn't pulled them apart.

"Please don't get this bitch back in her feelings." He fixed Rain's dress and playfully dusted off her face.

Rain ducked back and swatted at his hand. "Stop playing, boy."

"I'm just saying, hoe. You been acting a damn fool these past few days, and I know how people get when they're in their feelings. Any sign of affection will have your ass crying, and I got enough problems of my own. I'm not here for that shit today."

Rain and Fallon laughed at how dramatic he was being.

Fallon shook her head at Alex. "You are so crazy."

"He is." Rain looked at her. "What you doing in there?"

"Girl, I came out here with my sister-in-law and her man to get some food. They're supposed to be grilling out today. Y'all should come." She looked as if the idea had just popped into her head.

Alex shook his head immediately. "Nah, I don't think so. I don't know them."

"They're cool, Alex. You'll like them. It's just something to do. Jazz is at the house with her sister and kids right now. Us three just ran to the store to grab some meat."

"I'm good, but you can take your depressed ass sister-in-law if you want."

"Don't pass me off like I'm some kind of charity case."

Alex shrugged and looked past Fallon and to the entrance of the store. "Rain, ain't that Damien?" He pointed.

Rain and Fallon both looked toward the door. "Yes, that's him. Y'all know him?" Fallon asked.

"Yeah, that's Love's friend," Rain hurried to say. "They're real tight."

Fallon looked shocked. "Oh wow. The world is small. That's my sister-in-law's man."

Now the mention of his woman piqued Rain and Alex's attention. They had been trying to see this baby mama for a while now. Alex elbowed Rain discreetly when Damien stopped and grabbed the hand of the thick light-skinned girl that had just walked out of the store.

"Let me go see if they're okay with y'all coming. Y'all stay right here. I'll be right back." Fallon began to walk away. "Don't leave."

They weren't that far away from each other, so their voices could be heard clear as day. Rain could hear Fallon telling them about her and Alex. Damien mumbled something about he didn't care, but she wasn't surprised because he wasn't paying them any attention. He was so busy on his phone he hadn't even looked up yet. Rain was still being nosey, trying to hear what they were saying when she heard Fallon's sister-in-law tell her she was cool, and would be more than happy to meet her brother and his friends. Though that was nice of her, Rain had no intentions of accepting her invitation. That was it. It was time to go.

"Alex, let's go. I don't want to go over there."

"Why you ain't just tell her that?" Alex was busy snapping pictures of Damien and his baby mama. "We could have just spoke and then left." He was itching to be messy. It was all in his voice.

"Just come on before she comes back."

"Come on, bitch, damn. I wanted Damien to see me."

Rain could hear Alex talking, but she was already halfway to his truck. When he noticed she was gone, he took off in a light jog and met her there. He hit the locks and they hopped in.

"Let's ride back by so he can see me. I'll just tell her we ain't coming." Alex cranked up and was about to back out, but Rain grabbed his hand.

"No. Just pull off."

Alex looked over at her and for the first time, he noticed how uncomfortable she looked.

"What's wrong with you?"

"Damien's baby mama..." She looked at him with fear in her eyes. "She's the girl that attacked me."

To Be Continued...

Join our mailing list to get a notification when Leo Sullivan Presents has another release!

Text LEOSULLIVAN to 22828 to join!

To submit a manuscript for our review, email us at leosullivanpresents@gmail.com

CPSIA information can be obtained
at www.ICGtesting.com
Printed in the USA
LVHW081036091219
PP15473400001B/5/P